Praise for *I'm Still Here*

'A rare and beautiful novel. Simply this: a girl in a coma can hear, but nobody knows . . . [An] eloquent and romantic translated novel.'
Daily Mail

'A viscerally moving love story. *I'm Still Here* beautifully shows how the steady, quiet power of the heart can sustain anyone who takes on impossible odds.'
Sarah Pekkanen, author of *The Perfect Neighbours*

'Magnifique! With charming characters, a unique premise and a delightful, fresh voice, Clélie Avit's debut novel will have you cheering for life and love while you hungrily turn its pages. *I'm Still Here* is a gift, and Clélie Avit is a writer to watch.'
Julie Lawson Timmer, author of *Five Days Left*

CLÉLIE AVIT

I'm Still Here

Translated by Lucy Foster

HODDER

First published in Great Britain in 2016 by Hodder & Stoughton
An Hachette UK company

2

First published in paperback in 2017

A CIP catalogue record for this title is available from the British Library

Paperback ISBN 978 1 473 62676 8
Ebook ISBN 978 1 473 62675 1

Typeset in Plantin Light by Hewer Text UK Ltd, Edinburgh
Printed and bound by Clays Ltd, St Ives plc

Hodder & Stoughton policy is to use papers that are natural, renewable
and recyclable products and made from wood grown in sustainable
forests. The logging and manufacturing processes are expected to
conform to the environmental regulations of the country of origin.

Hodder & Stoughton Ltd
Carmelite House
50 Victoria Embankment
London EC4Y 0DZ

www.hodder.co.uk

To life, and love

I

Elsa

I'm cold. I'm hungry. I'm frightened.

At least, I think I am.

I've been in a coma for twenty weeks, so I assume I must be cold, hungry and frightened. Of course if anyone ought to know how I feel it's me, but for now all I can do is imagine.

I know I'm in a coma because I've heard them talking about it, distantly. I started hearing again six weeks ago, if my calculations are correct.

I count whatever I can. Though I've stopped counting the doctor's rounds; he hardly ever comes now. I counted nurses for a while, but they're pretty irregular too. The simplest thing is to count the cleaning lady's visits, because she comes into my room at about one in the morning every night. I know that because I hear the jangling of the radio that hangs from her trolley. I've counted it forty-two times.

Six weeks I've been awake.

Six weeks and nobody's noticed.

Of course I can't expect them to keep putting me through the brain scanner every five minutes. And if the monitor making the 'beep' noise beside me doesn't show that my brain is connected to my ears again, then why would they risk switching on such an expensive machine, just in case?

They all think I'm gone. Even my parents have started to let go. My mother doesn't come as often. Apparently my father stopped coming after ten days. Only my little sister comes regularly, every Wednesday, usually accompanied by her boyfriend of the moment.

She's like an overgrown teenager really, Pauline. Twenty-five years old and she still has a new beau almost every week. I wish I could whack her over the head sometimes to bring her to her senses but, as I can't, I just listen to her talk to me.

If there's one piece of advice the doctors love to give visitors, it's: 'Talk to her'. Every time I hear one of them say it (true, it happens less these days as they have less and less hope that I'll wake up), I feel like shoving their mint green scrubs down their scrawny necks. I don't know if they're even wearing mint green scrubs, but that's how I imagine them.

I imagine a lot of things.

I have nothing else to do. And, at the prospect of listening to my sister tell me all about her love life again, I sometimes allow my mind to wander. It's not that the details are especially boring, but she does tend to repeat herself. In fact all her stories are the same at the beginning, the same in the middle, and the same again at the end. The only thing that changes really is the guy's name. They're always students, always bikers, and there's always something very obviously dodgy about them. But she still hasn't noticed this, and I haven't told her. If I ever get out of this coma, I promise I'll let her know.

The one good thing about my sister's visits is when she talks to me about where I am. It only takes five minutes, the first five minutes after she comes into my room. She might talk about anything – the colour of the walls, the weather outside, the cut of the nurses' skirts, the grumpy porter she collided with on her way in – but she's studying Fine Art, so everything she describes is like hearing a poem of images. But that only lasts a few minutes and then we're off into a Mills and Boon novel for the next hour.

Today, apparently, it's grey outside and that makes the insipid walls of my room look even more awful than usual. The nurse is wearing a dreary beige skirt, just to liven things up. The man of the moment is called Adrien, but I switch off at the mention of his name and don't tune back in until the door has closed behind her.

Alone again.

I've been alone for twenty weeks, though I've only known it for six. Even so, it feels like an eternity. Perhaps it would pass quicker if I spent more time asleep, if my mind would switch off. But I don't like being asleep.

You see I'm actually not sure if I have any power over myself at all. I only seem to be capable of 'on' or 'off' mode, like an electrical appliance. My mind does pretty much whatever it wants. I'm like a squatter in my own body.

I don't like being asleep, because when I sleep I am somehow even further removed; I'm just a spectator. All these images file past me and I can't escape them in the way you normally would, by waking yourself up, tossing and turning, tangling yourself in the sheets, or even by talking yourself out of it. I can only watch, helpless, as the visions pass, and wait for them to finish.

Every night it's the same dream. Every night I am forced to watch a technicolour slow-motion replay of the moments that put me here, in this hospital bed. And the worst part is that I know I brought it upon myself. Just me. Me and my *icy passion*, as my father calls it. I'm sure that's why he doesn't come and visit. He must think it's my fault. He's never been able to understand why I love the mountains. He always used to say I'd come to a sticky end up a mountain. So he probably felt as though he'd won some kind of battle when this accident happened. I, on the other hand, don't feel as though I've won or lost *anything*. I have no feeling at all. I just want to get out of the coma.

I want to feel, really feel, cold, hungry and frightened.

It's amazing what you learn about your body when you're in a coma. For example, the fact that fear is just a chemical reaction. I ought to be terrified every night when I relive my nightmare, but no: I just watch.

I watch myself get up at three in the morning in the chalet dormitory and wake up my climbing buddies. I watch myself half-heartedly eat my breakfast, and hesitate about finishing my cup of tea, not wanting a full bladder out on the glacier. I watch myself methodically pull on each item of clothing, one by one, until I am covered from head to toe. I zip up my windbreaker, put on my gloves, arrange my headlamp and attach my crampons. I watch myself laughing with my friends, who are half asleep like me, but also somehow euphoric with the joy and adrenaline of the climb to come. I watch myself adjust my harness, throw the rope to Steve, and tie my figure-of-eight knot.

That figure-of-eight knot.

I must have tied it thousands of times.

That morning, I didn't get Steve to check it because he was in the middle of telling a joke – and it looked fine to me.

But now it's too late to warn myself. So I just watch as I wind the surplus rope onto one hand, taking my ice axe in the other, and set out. I watch myself panting, smiling, shivering, and walking. I walk and walk and walk, and then I walk some more. I advance cautiously. I see myself warning Steve to be careful as we approach the bridge of snow over the crevasse below. I see myself gritting my teeth as I go over the tricky part, and I see myself sigh with relief on the other side, and joke at how easy it was.

And then I see my legs give way under me.

I know the next part by heart. The bridge is just an enormous slab of snow, and I am the only one still left on it. The snow starts to slide, and I go with it. I feel the tug as the rope that joins me and Steve goes taut; we're like twins around an umbilical cord. There is relief at first, and then horror when the rope lengthens a few centimetres. I hear Steve, who is hanging from the ice, holding on with his crampons and ice axe. He shouts instructions, but the snow continues to fall, pressing down on my body. The tension around my waist relaxes, the knot gives way, and I fall.

I don't go far. Two hundred metres, perhaps. But the snow covers me all over. There is a terrible pain in my right leg and my wrists seem to be coming out at odd angles.

I feel as though I am asleep for a few seconds and then I wake up, more alert than I have ever been. My heart beats at top speed. I panic. I try to calm myself but it's difficult; I can't move any part of my body. The pressure is too great.

It's hard to breathe, even though there seems to be a small area of empty space in front of me. I open my mouth a little and, with difficulty, I gather the energy to cough. Saliva drips onto my right cheek. I must be on my side. I close my eyes and try to imagine myself at home in my bed, but it's impossible.

I hear footsteps above me, and Steve. I want to scream out. To tell him that I'm here, just under his feet. I hear other voices too. Must be the climbers we overtook earlier. I want to blow into my whistle, but that would mean moving my head and I can't. So I wait, frozen, petrified. Gradually the noises fade. I don't know if it's because they get further away, or because I'm asleep, but everything goes black.

And after that, the only thing I can remember is the voice of the doctor who tells my mother that there are more papers to fill in because they have moved me, 'because, you understand Madame, beyond fourteen weeks there is not much the medical team can do'.

This was when I realised I could only hear. I want to cry but I can't. I haven't even been able to muster the sad feeling you need in order to cry. I don't feel anything. I'm an empty shell.

Or a chrysalis in a rented cocoon – that's a bit prettier. But I'd really like to hatch and be a butterfly now, because this rented cocoon is also my body.

2

Thibault

'Leave me alone!'

'You're not going anywhere until you've seen him.'

'Just back off, will you. I've tried a thousand times already and nothing changes. He's a monster, he disgusts me. This all feels like some kind of fucked-up soap opera. I'm not going into that room.'

'He's your brother, for God's sake!'

'He was my brother before he ran over those two little girls, now he's just a person I don't want anywhere near me. Sometimes I wish he'd died out there with them, in the road. But I suppose he'll get what's coming to him.'

'Shit, Thibault, listen to yourself! You don't really mean that.'

I'm on a loop. I've been having the same conversation for the past month. My cousin thinks it's because I'm worried, but I'm not worried any more. I was at first, when the hospital called, when my mother collapsed on the kitchen floor, when we broke the speed limit all the way here in my cousin's old Peugeot 206. I was worried until the moment I saw the policeman outside my brother's room. And from that moment on, I've just been angry.

'Yes, I mean every word.'

I say this slowly, as cool as a cucumber. Apparently it's not what my cousin was expecting. He stops still in the corridor. My mother has already gone into room 55. A group of nurses walk past us, unfazed. I look at my cousin; he is horrified at me.

'Just stop getting so worked up and leave me to sort this out for myself. Tell Mum whatever you like, make up an excuse. I'll see you on the way out.'

I turn around, open the door that leads to the staircase and slam it behind me. Nobody ever uses the stairs in a hospital, so I exhale, close my eyes, and let myself slide slowly down the wall to the floor.

The polished concrete is cold through my jeans, but I don't care. My feet are already frozen from the unheated car journey and my fingertips have gone blue. Time to get my gloves out again. It's still autumn, officially, but there's a winter chill in the air. I can feel the bile rising in my throat, as I do every time I set foot in this hospital. I want to throw up my brother, his accident, the alcohol he slept off in that hospital bed the day after running down the two girls. My throat tightens in spasms but nothing comes out. Even the air here makes me sick. The smell of the hospital invades my nostrils. Odd: it's not normally as strong on the staircase. I need to get out of here as well.

I have opened a door and come into a room. But not the right one. I must have confused the sign in the corridor with one for an emergency exit. I'd better leave quickly before the person in the bed wakes up. I can only see the lower part of the legs from where I'm standing. Actually I can only see the pink sheet that is covering them. It smells of hospitals in here too, but something else catches my attention, a different smell that seems very far away from the medicine and disinfectant of these places. I close my eyes to concentrate.

Jasmine. It smells of jasmine. Very faint, but I'm certain. It's exactly like the tea my mother drinks in the mornings.

Strange that the noise from the door didn't wake this person up. I'm pretty sure they're still asleep. I'm not sure if it's a man or a woman but, judging by the fragrance, I'd say it must be a woman. I don't know many guys who use jasmine perfume.

I tiptoe forward carefully, hiding like a naughty kid behind the wall of the little bathroom. The smell of jasmine is stronger as I get closer. I put my head around the side.

A woman. No surprise there, but it was worth checking. She's fast asleep. Perfect. I'll be able to sneak out without anyone noticing.

As I creep back in the other direction I catch my reflection in the little mirror on the wall. Wild eyes, messy hair. My mother is always saying that I'd be more handsome if I sorted out my hair. When I tell her that I don't have time, she usually tells me that there would be 'girls lining up outside your door, if you would just tame that wild mane'. I tell her that I have better things to do than chat up girls, and she normally stops there.

Since I split up with Cindy a year ago, I've thrown myself into my work. Six years of sharing everything with someone has a big impact on the way you live, as it turns out. It hit me pretty hard when she left and I think I've been recovering ever since. So my hairstyle is not high on the list of priorities at the moment.

I probably ought to have a shave too. I don't look that bad, but I'm sure my mother would say I could do better. To listen to me, you'd think I spent all my time with my mother. I do have my own place, a couple of rooms on the third floor of a building with no lift. It's all right actually, and more importantly it's affordable. But my mother has been so upset this past month that I've been camping out in her living room a lot. She moved house when my father left, so she doesn't have a spare room any more. In fact I bought her the sofa bed – I must have had a premonition that it would come in handy one day. That was two months before Cindy left me.

I rub my rough cheeks vigorously, as though it will help to warm my fingers, then I tug at the collar of my sweater and pull the hem down in an attempt to give it some sort of shape. I can't believe I've been walking around like this all day at work and no one has said anything. They must know that Wednesday is visiting day. Maybe they saw the look in my eyes and knew to keep quiet – out of courtesy, or out of indifference. Or because they're hoping I'll have a nervous breakdown and get fired and then they can take my place.

There have been a few comments and funny looks at work since the day I lost it in the corridor and screamed at Cindy about sleeping with her boss. But since then she's moved to another office, and, in spite of my occasional outbursts, I'm one of the best employees they've got so I don't think they'd want to lose me.

My grey eyes look back at me in the mirror, pale against the mop of black hair. In a gesture of cooperation with my mother, I put a hand to my head and try to pat it down, but it doesn't work. Anyway, what's the point? I've got no one to impress.

A light tapping sound turns my attention towards the window. Damn. It's raining. I don't want to go back outside now to freeze and get soaked while I wait for my mother and my cousin. I look around. This room is nice and warm. The person is still asleep and, judging by the perfectly arranged furniture, it doesn't look as though she has many visitors.

I consider the situation for a moment. If she wakes up, I can always just tell her I came in by accident – she doesn't have to know that I decided to stay anyway. And if anyone comes to visit her, I can say I'm an old friend and then quickly make myself scarce. Better find out what her name is first though.

The clipboard at the foot of the bed says: 'Elsa Bilier, 29, head injury, severe trauma to the wrists and right knee. Multiple contusions, partially healed right fibula fracture . . .' The list continues until it reaches the most awful word of all.

'Coma.'

So there's no danger of her waking up, in fact. I put the clipboard down and take a look at this woman. Twenty-nine years old. With all the tubes and wires coming out of her in every direction, she could be a forty-or fifty-year-old, trapped in the middle of a spider's web. But on closer inspection, she does look twenty-nine. A pretty face, fine features, blonde hair, a few freckles here and there, a beauty spot by her right ear. She could be asleep; it's really only the thinness of her arms over the sheets and her hollow cheeks that give her away.

I look at the clipboard again and my breath catches.

Date of accident: 10 July.

She's been like this for nearly five months. I should put the clipboard back, but my curiosity gets the better of me.

Cause of injuries: glacial mountaineering accident.

It takes all sorts. I've never understood why anyone would go and risk life and limb out on a glacier, those freezing places full of hidden holes and weak spots where you might be about to die every time you take a step forward. I bet she's sorry now. Well, in a manner of speaking. I don't suppose she actually has any idea what's happened to her. That's how a coma works, isn't it? You go somewhere else and nobody knows how to bring you back.

Suddenly I have a terrible urge to swap her with my brother. Stuck in there all alone. She hasn't hurt anyone, at least I doubt it. Whereas my brother drank too much, got behind the wheel and killed two fourteen-year-old girls. He's the one who should still be in a coma. Not her. I look at the clipboard one last time before putting it back.

Elsa. Twenty-nine. Date of birth: 27 November.

Wait, it's her birthday today.

I don't know why I do it, but I take the pencil tied to the clipboard and rub out the '29'. It makes a dirty smear but who cares.

'You're thirty today, gorgeous,' I murmur as I write in the new number, before putting the clipboard back.

I look at her again. Something about her is making me uncomfortable and, after a moment, I know what it is. Being linked up to all these machines demeans her somehow. If I disconnected it all she'd look almost like a jasmine flower, with the smell to match. To disconnect or not to disconnect, that is the question. I've never thought about it before. But right now I would love to remove all her tubes just to make her look normal.

'Look how pretty you are – you deserve a birthday kiss.'

My words surprise me, but I've already started moving aside the tubes that block the way to her cheek. Up close, the smell of jasmine is very distinct. I put my lips on her warm cheek and it gives me something like an electric shock.

It's been a year since I last gave someone a kiss, except for greeting work colleagues or friends, but that doesn't count. There's nothing especially sensual in what I've just done, but it was a stolen kiss from the cheek of an unsuspecting woman. The idea makes me smile and I stand back.

'You're lucky it's still raining, jasmine flower. I'm going to keep you company for a little while longer.'

I pull the chair over and sit down. It takes me about two minutes to fall asleep.

3

Elsa

I am desperate to feel something – anything – but I feel absolutely nothing.

If I believe everything I hear, though, someone has been in my room for about ten minutes. A man. A man of about thirty, I'd guess. A non-smoker as far as I can make out from his voice. But that's as much as I can say.

And I can only take his word for it when he says that he kissed me, because I didn't feel it.

What did I expect? The Sleeping Beauty effect? Prince Charming turns up, gives me a kiss and whoosh, here I am, ta-da!

'Hi Elsa, I'm whatsisname, I have woken you up; now let us be married.'

If I believed that I'd have set myself up for a cruel disappointment, because of course nothing like that has happened. It's far less interesting; more like: 'Hi, I'm a bloke who wandered into your room by accident [well, I assume he did, otherwise I have no idea what he's doing here] and I'm going to shelter until the rain has stopped and I can go back outside.' Now he's already breathing deeply in the chair beside me.

I'm curious – curiosity isn't chemical, so I can still

recognise it when it happens – I'm curious to know who is sitting in the chair beside my bed. I have no way of finding out, so I make it up. Until now, apart from doctors, nurses and the cleaning lady, the only people who ever came into this room were people I knew. I had to imagine what they might be wearing, but that was it. This one's a real challenge because I have nothing to go on aside from his voice.

And I like his voice. It makes a change, at least. It's the first new voice I've heard in six weeks so I expect, even if it had been a hoarse drone, I'd probably still have liked it. My sister's boyfriends don't speak, or they stay out in the corridor. The only thing I hear from them, eventually, is the inevitable sound of their saliva being exchanged with my sister's. But this new voice has a unique quality, a mixture of lightness and passion.

And it has enabled me to confirm today's date.

I really have been here for five months, then, and today is my birthday.

The thing that surprises me about this new information is that my sister didn't mention it when she was here. Maybe she thought it was pointless. Or maybe she just forgot. I'd like to believe that, but I can't. A thirtieth birthday isn't something you just forget, is it?

There's a stirring next to me. I hear the movement of fabric on fabric and recognise it as the sound of a sweater being removed. There are little irregularities in his breath while he gets his arms out of the sleeves and pulls it over his chest, then his breathing pauses while he pulls it over his head. I hear the sweater being put down somewhere and then the breathing is regular again.

I am on full alert. At least I like to think that I am. All of my active parts, which are comprised solely of my hearing of course, are clinging to this new thing like a life raft. So I listen, I listen, I listen. And, bit by bit, I draw a portrait of him in my head.

His breathing is peaceful. He must have fallen asleep. The tapping of the rain on the window is light and, over it, I can make out the sound of his T-shirt moving steadily up and down over the plastic of the chair. He can't be very fat, or he wouldn't breathe like that. I try to compare this with the sound of the people I know, but we hardly ever listen to people breathe. I suppose I must have listened to ex-boyfriends a few times, if I've woken up before them. But they'd probably all have thought it was stupid. I do remember one guy who breathed at triple speed in his sleep. I wanted to laugh when I heard him, but I was frightened of waking him up. That relationship didn't last long.

My romances have always been chaotic, and far less regular and less numerous than my sister's. I'd guess there have been about ten, from memory. Some short, others longer. At the moment I'm single. It's better that way because who knows how a guy would have reacted to this coma. Would he have dumped me at the start? Would he have waited? Would he have moved on without saying anything to me at all? Would he have come in and told me that it was over? That wouldn't have been too hard; he'd probably have assumed I couldn't hear him anyway. And he would have been right for the first fourteen weeks.

So, I'm single and glad about it. It's hard enough to hear my mother crying every time she visits; I have no desire to duplicate the experience with anyone else.

Even as these things go through my mind, I stay focused on my accidental visitor. His breathing is deeper. He must be fast asleep.

I concentrate all my attention on him. I don't want the time to pass. He is my only distraction, the one novelty in all this time, practically the only thing that has reminded me that I really am alive in some small way.

Because I can't honestly say that Pauline's visits, or the nurses', or my mother and her sobbing, actually cheer me up. But this is like a pebble being thrown into the water, an actual change. This would make a ripple on my surface if only I could move.

I want time to stop, but it doesn't. I've only got this little siesta that he has allowed himself in my room. As soon as he leaves, everything will be as it was before. I'll just have to see it as a birthday present. I'd like to be able to smile at this thought.

I hear voices coming down the corridor, and my whole being lights up from the inside. It's Steve, Alex and Rebecca. They sound animated and happy. I have a sudden desire to tell them to be quiet, so they don't wake him up. But as usual I can't do anything, and actually I'm a little curious to see how my intruder is going to explain his presence.

The catch on the door squeaks and then the footsteps and voices all stop at once.

'Someone's already here!' exclaims Rebecca.

'Do you know him?' whispers Alex from behind her.

I suppose Rebecca shakes her head. I hear them come in, circling the chair, and I imagine them bending over my visitor to examine him.

'He's asleep – shall we just leave him and see if he wakes up?'

'No, let's get him out,' says Steve.

'Well, he's not bothering anyone,' says Rebecca, hesitant, 'and if he's a friend of Elsa's, he can celebrate with us, can't he?'

'Well . . .'

I can hear Steve's reluctance. I know he used to have a soft spot for me. Girls who are interested in climbing up glaciers don't grow on trees, even when you live near the Alps. Rebecca stopped three years ago, when she started getting too frightened. Perhaps I should have listened to her when she tried to persuade me to do the same. But no, I'm 'too passionate'. I could tell that Steve had fallen for me quite soon after we met, but I was with someone at the time, so I made it clear that I was only looking for a climbing buddy. My other friends were too tall, I needed someone my height. Steve is perfectly proportioned. We made a killer team.

As soon as he understood that I wasn't interested in him romantically, he cast himself in the role of big brother. It's nice to feel as though someone's looking out for you, when you're the eldest child. And since Alex and Rebecca have been together, Steve's protectiveness has gone into overdrive.

And that's exactly what he's doing now. Being the brother who won't let anyone near his little sister.

'Come on, Steve,' Alex starts. 'What do you think is going to happen in the hospital? He must just be a friend of Elsa's who's fallen asleep, that's all. Let's not make a big thing of it. The question is whether we wake him up, or start the party without him.'

'Looks like he's made the decision for us,' says Rebecca.

I hear my visitor wake up. I visualise his eyes opening, adjusting to their environment, and I want to laugh when I hear him gasp on discovering that there are three people watching him.

'Who are you?' Steve doesn't waste any time. I bet he's squared up to him, his face about ten centimetres away from the face of the stranger, eyes squinting, trying to recreate Superman's laser-beam stare. I count to five before my imposter replies, his voice still melodious.

'A friend.'

'Right . . .'

'Yes, right, I'm a friend.'

Confirmation that he must be at least thirty, or he wouldn't be this assured with Steve.

'I don't believe you.'

'Steve,' interrupts Alex, 'stop it.'

'I don't know him,' retorts Steve. 'It's already like going through airport security just to get onto this ward.

I want to know who he is and what he thinks he's doing here!'

'That's exactly why he can't be doing anything wrong here, if he's already managed to get in!'

'Right . . .'

My stranger straightens up and puts his sweater back on. 'Do you know how to say anything other than "Right . . ."?'

Whoa. He doesn't know what he's getting himself into. I'd like to warn him, but it's too late. It sounds as though Steve has grabbed him by the collar and pulled him out of the chair.

'Who do you think you are?'

'Steve, stop it!' cries Rebecca.

'Fucking hell, who does this guy think he is?' Steve says again.

'Let go of him!' says Alex. 'And you,' he turns to my visitor, 'should apologise – if not, we won't stick up for you a second time.' Alex, the perfect gentleman. I can see why Rebecca fell in love with him.

'I'm sorry,' says my visitor flatly. 'Will you let me go now?'

I can hear Steve's grumblings as he lets the stranger go. And then he sits beside me on the bed. The starched sheets rustle near my ear.

'Sorry, Elsa,' he murmurs, stroking my hair. 'That's it, I promise. Just a little excitement for your birthday.'

I hear his voice waver for a second or two. He blames himself for not having checked my knot, or for not having been strong enough to stop me falling with the avalanche.

From what I understand, it was Steve who got me out from under the snow. The doctor said it had been a miracle that he found me at all. But I know that it was the connection between us. A big brother always looks out for you.

Today, though, I have to admit that he's taking it a bit far.

'So! Elsa, we've brought you a cake, with thirty candles that you almost certainly wouldn't want to blow out, but I would force you to anyway. And we've got you a little present.' The sound of Rebecca's voice cheers me up. She empties out the contents of a plastic bag and I'm sure it's Alex who helps her to arrange the candles.

As they do this, my visitor gets up.

'You're sure that you're a friend of Elsa's?' Steve starts again where he left off. If I ever get out of this coma, I'm going to be having words with him about this.

'Yes.'

'So what's her name then?'

'Elsa. You've said it at least three times.'

'Her surname.'

'Bilier. And she's thirty today.'

'Rebecca's just given you that information.'

'Is this an interrogation or something?'

'Yes, you could say that.' Steve, the over-protector. 'What does she study?'

Two seconds pass before my stranger answers.

'She doesn't study. She works.'

'In what?'

Two seconds again.

'The mountains.'

I'm impressed. He's bluffing, but he does it well. Maybe we do know each other after all.

'And what does she do, exactly, in the mountains?'

I lose all hope that my stranger will guess this one. I've got an unusual job.

Ten long seconds pass. Alex and Rebecca are lighting the candles and I can hear them murmuring to each other. The stranger takes a few steps across the room and then stops. He must have turned back to Steve.

'OK,' he begins. 'You're right. I don't know Elsa. Everything I've just said, I guessed from what's written in her notes at the bottom of the bed. I'm just a visitor who came into the wrong room. It was quiet, I sat down for a minute. I wasn't bothering anyone. Now I'll leave.'

Oddly, Steve says nothing. It's Rebecca who speaks first.

'Don't you want to stay for the candles?'

My stranger must be surprised. Rebecca is like that, adorable and sometimes a bit naïve. But luckily her Prince Charming is always by her side.

'Stay for a bit,' says Alex.

'I don't want to get in your way,' replies the stranger.

'You said it yourself, you haven't bothered anyone. That'll make us four at the party, Elsa would love it.'

He must be hesitating. 'OK.'

The stranger comes over again and moves the chair. I have the impression that he tries to help Alex with something in a bag, while Rebecca picks up the clipboard at the bottom of my bed.

'It doesn't look as though there's been much progress,' she says to the others. 'There's nothing new on here at all. Oh, yes. Someone has changed her age. Impressive that they pay attention to things like that.'

'Uh . . . no, that was . . . I did that,' says the stranger. 'I looked at the papers to find out what she was called and I saw that it was her birthday today. I'm sorry if that was the wrong thing to do. I probably shouldn't have.'

'You're joking, right? That's so nice of you!'

'Really?'

'I think it's lovely that someone who doesn't even know Elsa would take the trouble to correct her age in her notes. OK, shall we get the present out now? I think Steve should open it, even though he knows exactly what's inside!'

Steve must have reached out for it and then turned to me. Rebecca puts the cake on the little table to one side. I imagine the smell of fruit, the light from the flames, and the sad smiles of my friends.

'Well . . . Happy birthday, my sweet,' says Rebecca before blowing out my thirty candles.

'Happy Birthday, Elsa,' says Alex.

'Happy Birthday, you,' says Steve.

From further away, the murmur of my stranger reaches my ears. 'Happy birthday.' He says it so quietly. I don't know if that's because he's embarrassed, or sad, or something else. But in any case, it's touching. Very touching.

'Here's your present,' says Steve, bringing me back to reality. 'It's a ring. You always said that you'd never marry anyone, and that no one should bother giving you a ring because you'd be annoyed, so we've got you one. Perhaps you'll come back quicker if you're desperate to kick our arses.' I suppose Steve has put it on one of my fingers. I don't know which hand, let alone which finger.

'Aren't you going to tell her what it looks like?' My stranger's interruption seems to surprise everyone. 'I mean, I don't know,' he continues. 'But if you're going to speak to her, you might as well tell her everything, don't you think?'

The silence lasts for several moments.

'You can do the honours,' Steve mumbles, as though he wishes he had thought of it himself.

'Uh . . .'

'Go on. You're right!'

'Well . . . OK.'

My visitor comes closer. 'Well, it's silver.'

'It's white gold,' Steve corrects him.

'Oh, sorry. I don't know the difference.'

'It's more durable.'

'OK. So, it's white gold. They chose it because it's more durable, so if you bash it with your . . . ice axe, it'll still be fine.'

I'd like to laugh, or at least smile at his little show of climbing expertise.

'There are two intertwining strands which go all the way round. Sort of like vines. Or maybe like the stalk of a flower. Ah! Or like a jasmine flower, because you seem to like the smell.'

I'm amazed. How on earth does he know that?

'How do you know that?'

Thanks, Steve.

'It smells of jasmine all over this room. And it comes from her.'

'Are you a perfume expert or something?'

'No, I'm an ecologist – no connection. Shall I carry on?'

'Sure.'

I realise that I'm impatient to hear what's coming next.

'It shines. And it looks very pretty. And it's on your right ring finger.'

I'm a bit disappointed. I almost want Steve to interrupt him again.

'Apart from that, the cake is pear,' he continues, 'and Rebecca was lying, she put thirty-one candles on it, just to annoy you, and I can tell that you've got some true friends here, for coming to celebrate your birthday with you even after you've abandoned them for almost five months.'

At this, the silence turns heavy. For a minute I'm frightened that my hearing has gone. But the sound of the raindrops tapping on the window reassures me. I hear someone blow their nose. I think it's Rebecca. I imagine Alex putting his arms around her. Everyone is looking for something to do to dissipate the sadness which must have invaded the room. Pieces of cake circulate, spoons hit against the paper plates.

'Can you tell us more about you?' asks Rebecca after a moment.

'What do you want to know?' replies my visitor.

'You could start by introducing yourself, perhaps. We only know how you got here. I'm curious to know more about a person who can learn so much about someone they don't know in less than five minutes.'

'My name is Thibault. I'm thirty-four. And I'm supposed to be with my brother who's had a car accident.'

'Oh gosh, I hope it wasn't too serious,' says Rebecca.

'It was. He'll get better, but I'd prefer it if he didn't, to be honest. He killed two teenagers in the accident, because he was drunk. I don't really ever want to see him again.'

'Ah.'

The silence returns. I reflect on what I've just heard. I'm getting more of an idea about my stranger, but there are still some vital details missing. Unfortunately I doubt that any of my friends will ask him to describe himself to me.

Thibault. I must remember that name.

'How did she get here?' he asks suddenly. 'Aside from the "glacial mountaineering", I mean.'

Steve gets up. He paces up and down the room and tells the part of the story that I already know. I listen carefully to what follows, from the moment they found me. I learn an important new detail: I was helicoptered out. What a shame – I've always dreamed of a helicopter ride over that glacier and when my chance came I wasn't conscious to see it. My visitor asks questions, just as I hoped. I would love to have been able to reply to them myself . . .

'Why does she do it? I mean, why does she climb glaciers? It's pretty risky isn't it, all that stuff?'

'It's in her blood,' says Steve.

'That doesn't sound like enough of a reason to me,' replies Thibault.

'Do you know what happiness is?'

'Is that a trick question?'

'Elsa knows,' says Steve, ignoring him. 'When she gets up there, she is herself completely. She glows. The mountain is her element. It's a vocation, as well as a passion.'

'So, she's a guide?'

'No, she'd never do that. She works for the organisation that makes the hiking maps. She's a specialist in glacial areas.'

'I didn't know that job existed. Even though I've probably used some of those maps.'

'Well, there you go. Elsa *is* the mountains. When you walk across a mountain with her it's like seeing her *and it* stripped bare. Open to possibilities. All her emotions are raw. She's wonderful.'

'Wow . . . are you in love?'

That was a sincere question. And after all that Steve has just said, I'm also waiting for his response.

'I was. Now I'm just a sort of big brother who's failed in his mission.'

'Don't say that,' Thibault says immediately. 'There was nothing you could have done if her figurate knot wasn't tied properly.'

'Figure *of eight*,' corrects Steve. 'But I should have checked it.'

Rebecca breaks the silence by collecting the plates and spoons.

It is the end of the little birthday party and my visitor is about to leave.

'Well, thank you for the cake, and for letting me stay.'

'Are you sure you won't stay a bit longer?' suggests Alex.

'No, I'm going to go and find my mother and my cousin. They're probably looking for me by now.'

'OK. It was good to meet you.'

'You too. Say goodbye to her from me.'

'You can do it yourself,' says Rebecca.

He seems to hesitate, but then I hear him approach. He was more confident earlier, when we were alone together.

'We kiss her forehead,' explains Rebecca. 'It's the only place where there aren't too many tubes.'

'Oh, right.'

I hear the noise of his lips on my skin but, as before, I don't feel anything. I hear him whisper in my ear, as discreetly as possible, before stepping back.

'Goodbye, Elsa.'

He moves away from my bed. The others carry on in the background.

'Thanks again; I'm off.'

'You can come and see her again, whenever you like, you know.' It is Alex who makes this suggestion, of course.

'Oh. That's kind. Thank you. I don't know whether . . .'

'You'd be very welcome,' adds Rebecca. 'She'd be so pleased to have other people coming to visit her. I'm certain.'

'Great, OK. Bye then.'

The door closes. My visitor is gone. And my happiness is gone with him.

'Steve?' says Alex. 'You haven't said anything for a while. Did it bother you that I suggested he come again?'

'No, it's fine.'

'So what's up?'

'It's just that it's started snowing and Elsa would have loved that.'

The sadness weighs down each of his words. I think I preferred it when it was just Thibault in here. There was less emotion. I listen to my friends getting their things together and putting their coats on. I hear them kiss me on the forehead one by one, with no hope of responding to them.

When the door closes gently, I am left in total silence again. Not even rain against the window now. No one's breathing but mine.

I'd like him to come back.

4
Thibault

My mother is looking at my reflection in the car window and my cousin is playing with his phone in the back seat. I drive mechanically towards my mother's apartment. I know the route by heart, but I should be paying more attention to the road.

Impossible when my mind is elsewhere.

In that room. Room 52. I checked the number on my way out. There was a photo of a mountain on the door, sublime-looking, covered in ice. It must have been the picture that lured me in there.

When I got to the ground floor of the hospital, my cousin was already there waiting for me. He tried to find out what I'd been doing. Of course I didn't say a word. When my mother came out a few minutes later her eyes were red. She's calmer now. That hospital is like an enormous magnet for everyone's tears.

I want to drop her off as quickly as possible. I find myself less and less able to cope with all her emotion. It's not that I blame her, not at all. She has every right to be upset. I'm sure I'd be in the same state if it was my child in a hospital bed, but compared to the situation in room 52, my brother is almost like a placebo case on that ward.

This afternoon has been more eventful than expected. I just went for a nap and now suddenly there's a whole world of new information in my head. They were all right, those three. Even Steve, behind his over-protective big brother pose; he was just worried. And sad. A bit like my mother. That was what most got on my nerves about him: the tortured sadness thing. He seemed jealous too, but I don't know what he could have been jealous of. If he's genuinely not in love with her, then I don't pose any threat. And even if he is in love, he still has nothing to worry about from me.

The girl, Rebecca, was sweet – a bit naïve perhaps, but nice. And I thought her boyfriend Alex seemed like a good guy too; friendly. It was almost worth wandering in there just to meet them. I hardly ever meet new people these days. But I realise that there's actually no way of making friends with them, apart from perhaps leaving a note in room 52, saying: 'Hi, it's Thibault, the guy who fell asleep in here the other day. If you'd like to hang out again, here's my number.' That would be nuts.

The only person I can see again, if I want, is the one who I can't speak to. Or at least who doesn't answer back.

Elsa, the jasmine flower covered in pipes and tubes. I didn't ask them why there were so many. I know absolutely nothing about medicine. Although I do work in 'earth medicine', as I've heard some people call it, when it comes to the human body, I've got no idea. When my brother's doctor tried to explain his injuries to me, I zoned out after a couple of seconds. My mother listened patiently, even though she didn't understand any of it either. My cousin, who's a PE teacher, gave us a rough translation afterwards. But, to be honest, the sight of the policeman waiting behind the door had already made my blood run cold, so I couldn't really listen properly.

Thankfully there's no policeman any more. My brother made a statement, confessing his guilt. His sentencing will be in four months. Technically, that's the length of time it should take him to recover from the accident. In the meantime, his apartment is sitting empty. My cousin and I went over to clear out the fridge and tidy up, so that it didn't get too disgusting while he was away. It wasn't exactly a palace to begin with, so it wouldn't have taken long for it to start to feel like a slum. While we were there we discovered that he had a girlfriend, or at least there was a girl's underwear strewn about all over the place. But this girl, whoever she is, hasn't been worried enough to contact us about him, so it can't be very serious.

I park in the space in front of my mum's building. The snow is starting to show on the parked cars. It hasn't settled on the tarmac, but there is a fine dusting of it on the grass, so I suppose if it carries on the roads will be dangerous. I can't say that I either like or dislike snow. It's there. I take it for what it is. To me, it's just another way that the planet breathes and carries out its functions.

My two passengers get out of the car. My cousin lives just next to my mum. He's the one who found the place for her when my father left. I feel the car lift a little, without the weight of them in it. My cousin puts his head back through the window.

'Are you coming in?'

'Not tonight.'

'I think she'd appreciate it, Thibault.'

'I can't face it tonight.'

'You're a selfish fucker, you know that.'

'Hey, I'll come tomorrow. I just . . . can't tonight.'

My cousin looks at me, almost in surprise that I have conceded to coming again tomorrow.

'OK. Drive carefully.'

My mother looks at me from outside and waves. I blow her a kiss and switch the engine back on. I start to feel better as soon as I've gone back through the entrance gate of the apartment block. I spend so much time with them, the misery weighs me down. It's like I'm a sponge, soaking it up.

I begin to drive automatically again until I realise that I'm going in the wrong direction, back towards town. Perhaps that's where I should go. I don't want to be alone tonight, but I don't really want company either. Tough one. Luckily, I know who to call.

'Jules? Hi – I'm driving so I shouldn't talk. But what are you doing tonight? Do you fancy a drink? That's fine, I can wait . . . See you a bit later then, thanks buddy.'

Julien, former work addict, and now addicted to his five-month-old daughter, has been my best friend for as long as I can remember. By coincidence, his wife Gaëlle was one of my best mates at college, so she'll understand him coming out to see me. As far as I could understand, he was still in the midst of the bath-time and bottle-feeding ritual. Wednesday is his day, I'd forgotten. They seem to live in perfect harmony, those two. I'm jealous, though

I'm not looking for anyone at the moment. But if I did ever find someone, that's how I'd like it to be: balanced.

With Cindy there was no balance; it was a thunder-storm every single day. I used to excuse it by saying that what we had was a different sort of equilibrium. But that was just bullshit. When I see what those two have achieved, I wish I had it. But, coming from the relationship I just got out of, who knows if I'm even still capable of love.

So, in the meantime I love my work, I love my friends, I love my mum, even if she is constantly blubbing. But I can't love my brother any more. That's where I always get stuck.

Oh, and I hate the idiots who don't park properly in the free spaces. Because of their enormous gaps I'm obliged to go and pay for a space in the car park.

Though it's more expensive, I choose the place that's closest to the pub where Julien and I always go. I'll have about two hundred metres to walk, at the most, which is perfect because it's freezing outside now that it's dark. I position the car extremely carefully, so as not to be a parking hypocrite, and place the ticket methodically in my pocket so that I don't do the same thing I did last time, which was spend two hours hunting all over for the ticket because I'd left it on the dashboard. Then I run into the pub.

Inside it's warm. There are people talking, laughing, music playing, and I find a free table. It's a relief to be in a place where no one is crying. I sit down and put two beer mats on the table opposite me, to show that I'm waiting for someone. These unwritten rules reassure me. And this way no one needs to ask if the seat is free or not.

I ask for a pineapple juice. The barman looks at me, perplexed. I tell him that I'm driving and that seems to satisfy him. He almost congratulates me, even. I expect Julien will order a beer when he arrives. I have a few drinks now and again, but never when I'm driving. If only my brother were the same.

I haven't had my pineapple juice in my hand for more than five minutes when a girl comes and sits down opposite me.

'Is this chair free?'

I indicate the beer mats, exasperated.

'Oh sorry, I didn't see. Are you waiting for someone?'

'Yes. A friend.'

I want to say 'my girlfriend', or even 'my boyfriend', because this girl's flirtatious manner is so shameless I'd like to scare her off. But I don't. This is normally a relaxed pub, not a pick-up joint. I smile, thinking of what my mother says about my appearance. Obviously someone likes my messy hair. Although she might just be after a free drink. I'm always so uncomfortable with this type of encounter.

'How would you like it if I kept you company until he arrives?'

I'm bound to say the wrong thing, so I have a sort of gamebook in my head, which I turn to when I need advice. I call it, snappily, *The Book in Which I Am the Hero*. It opens now: If you want to fight the dragon, go to page 62. If you'd rather hide, go to page 33. Without warning, it flicks to the last option, page 0.

'Look, I can see you're pretty out of it, but I'm still amazed that you can't tell whether someone is inviting you to sit down or not. I know these things can be quite subtle, and I'm not sure that subtlety is your thing – but either way, just to be clear, I definitely don't want you to keep me company until my mate arrives, thanks all the same.'

The girl is outraged, and I actually wonder whether she still quite understood what I said. Looking at her, she doesn't seem used to being knocked back, but I'm not in the mood to mess around.

Presumably she goes off and tells everyone in the pub what an arsehole I am, either that or the beer mats on the table do work, because no one else bothers me until Julien arrives. It's almost eight. He's got snow in his hair when he comes in.

'Phew! What a day!' he exclaims and sits down opposite me.

'It's just snow,' I say.

'But it's freezing,' he says, taking off his gloves.

'Tell me about it . . .'

He takes off his jacket and signals that he'd like a beer. I lift my empty pineapple juice glass and the guy behind the counter nods his head.

'So, what's going on?' Julien asks in a serious voice.

'Oh you know, it's Wednesday.'

'Your day to visit your brother, right? But you do go on other days as well, don't you?'

'Just to take my mother.'

'So you still don't want to see him?'

'No.'

'What's wrong?'

'Why are you asking me that?'

'Thibault, it's written all over your face. And you'd never have called me at six on a Wednesday, which you know is my day to put Clara to bed, if it wasn't important.'

'How is Clara? I hope I haven't got you into trouble with Gaëlle . . .'

'Don't worry, Gaëlle took over, no problem, and Clara's good. Healthy – the paediatrician said she's doing really well. It's still OK for you to be her godfather, isn't it?'

'Yes, of course it's still OK. She's an angel, that baby. How could I possibly change my mind? If she carries on like this I might even have to marry her!'

'Pff,' laughs Julien. 'So it's a girl thing, then.'

'No. Well . . . maybe. But it's not what you think.'

'So what's this all about?'

I put my glass down and sink back into my chair.

'It's about a girl, some of her friends, my brother, the police, lots of tubes, jasmine and our car journeys to and from the hospital.'

'Wow! I didn't understand any of that.'

The waiter comes over with Julien's beer and my pineapple juice. We thank him. I fill my glass again, spill some on the table and wipe it up clumsily.

'Could you elaborate, please?' he asks.

'Yup, hang on.' My hands are sticky so I get a tissue out of my pocket. I always have tissues with me these days, since I've been taking my mother to the hospital – someone's bound to be crying somewhere. 'It's a thing that happened to me earlier today.'

I tell him about my afternoon. He is quiet all the way through, listening patiently. When I've finished he just looks at me.

'You're not going to say anything?'

'Well, what do you want me to say?' he says at last. 'It's pretty funny.'

'Funny? That's not exactly the word I would have chosen.'

'Well, puzzling, bizarre, weird then, is that better? The thing that interests me is why this has had such an effect on you. You went into the wrong room, that's all!'

He waits for me to explain. As an answer, he's going to get the question that I've had in my head for the last three hours.

'Why do I wish I could swap this girl's situation with my brother's?'

Julien is getting worried. I can see it in his eyes.

'You mean you'd like her to wake up and your brother to be in a coma?'

'Exactly.'

'You know why that is.'

'No I don't.'

'Stop, Thibault. You still can't accept the fact that your brother ran over those two girls. And, frankly, no one would want you to. In your place I'd feel the same. This girl, Elsa, seems nice and you'd like her to wake up, as anyone would. You've got a heart! It's normal to feel like this.'

'A heart . . . I never want to see my own brother again and you still think I have a heart?'

'Everyone has a heart, Thibault. But it's what they do with it that counts. Yours was in a thousand pieces after Cindy. And now it's in a million pieces since the accident. You're telling yourself that if there was something you could do to wake this girl up, it might help you to gather a few of the pieces. You just need to forgive yourself for having negative thoughts about your brother.'

I'm flabbergasted, but that's why Julien is my best friend. It's such a relief to hear him say it that, for the first time in a year, I can feel my eyes filling with tears. But I can't cry in here. Not in a crowded pub. Not on a Wednesday night.

'Come on, let's go,' says Julien.

'What?'

'Let's get out of here, Thib.'

He drains his glass and makes me finish mine. Two minutes later, we're out on the snowy pavement. He was right, it's freezing. Julien takes my arm and pulls me a bit further from the door. I stumble; my eyes have gone blurry, and it's not just the snow.

'It's OK,' he says to me.

I break down. Two blokes holding onto each other outside a pub, that's not something you see every day. You'd assume we were gay, I suppose. Well, if anyone comes past they can assume what they like. I just want to cry out all the water obstructing my vision. I want to spit out all the saliva from my mouth. I want to scream out in despair so that everyone can hear me.

I content myself with crying into Julien's shoulder and he draws me closer to him. I realise that it's several months since I have been this close to another body, and the warmth of an old friend is very comforting. We stand like this for several minutes, then the cold takes over. Julien hands me a tissue. He always has them on him too, because of the baby.

'Come back to mine,' he says.

'Sorry?'

'You're coming to stay at ours tonight, I'm not letting you go home in this state.'

'I haven't been drinking, I won't run anyone over.'

'I know that! You've always been the sober one, Thibault, and now more than ever, but you're too miserable to be on your own tonight. Where's the car?'

'In the car park over there.'

'OK, I walked over, so you can give me the keys and I'll drive us back.'

I do as he says without protesting, follow him to the car park and pay for the exit ticket. Then I get into the passenger seat. It feels strange to be in the passenger in my own car.

Julien is a steady driver. I let myself be rocked by the car's motion. He doesn't live far away so we're there quickly. When we get in, Gaëlle comes to the door smiling.

'Thibault!' she whispers. The little one must be asleep.

'Hi Gaëlle,' I say, smiling. 'I'm sorry for the intrusion.'

'Don't apologise,' she says, kissing my cold cheeks. 'Julien warned me on the phone. I've made your bed in Clara's room. Just don't snore too loudly. And I'm afraid you might be woken up at 4 a.m. when she wants her bottle.'

'I don't mind, she's my little princess. But . . . Julien warned you? When did you do that?' I ask, turning towards him.

'By text message while you were bawling into my shoulder.'

'You bastard, I thought you were sharing in my distress!'

'You were in the process of ruining my jacket, I had to act quickly.'

'When you two have finished,' interrupts Gaëlle, 'there's some food in the kitchen. Thibault, I left a towel on your bed, in case you want a shower.'

'Thanks Gaëlle, this is so kind of you.'

'You'd do the same for us,' she says.

'Thanks all the same.'

I take off my jacket and my shoes while they exchange a quick kiss and a couple of updates about the baby. Gaëlle says I can go and see Clara and put down my things because she's not asleep yet.

Walking into the room is like stepping across into another dimension. This used to be Julien's office, but now he's moved everything out into the living room. The sofa bed has been moved in here and there's just a non-folding sofa in the living room, because it would be impossible to open out a mattress in the space that's left.

The apartment is not very big, but they've saved the best spot for their daughter. I lean over the cot. Clara watches me come in as though I'm an alien. She wiggles her fingers and beams up at me with her glowing, angelic face. Gaëlle and Julien really have done a good job with this one.

I look around. The sofa bed is out. The duvet and pillow look very inviting, much more inviting than that girl in the pub. I leave the room quietly and pull the door closed behind me. Gaëlle is watching television in the living room and Julien is waiting for me in the kitchen.

I hesitate before sitting down, but after all that crying I realise that I'm absolutely starving. During dinner we talk about everything and nothing. Quite a lot about Clara – it's so easy for a child to become the main focus. I do the washing-up with Julien, and Gaëlle tells us that she's going to bed. She'll have to be up when the baby cries for her bottle. I suggest that I give Clara the bottle tonight so that she can sleep.

'Would you?'

'With pleasure. I need to practise if I'm going to be her godfather, don't I?'

'That would be wonderful, thank you. Then we could have a whole night's sleep.'

'So where's all the equipment?' I ask, looking around the kitchen.

'It's all there,' she says, motioning to a corner of the work surface. 'You just need to put this in the bottle-warmer.'

Gaëlle kisses us both and goes into the bedroom. I tell Julien I'm going to have a shower. The hot water does me good. I'm in there a while, even though I know it's not good for the environment. It is helping, and I've been feeling like crap, so the planet will have to wait, for today . . .

When I come out, Julien tells me that he's going to bed too. I sit in front of the TV for a while and then turn everything off. I don't have a book with me, but I'm not sure I'd be in the mood for reading anyway.

I go quietly into Clara's room and slide under the duvet. The covers are freezing. I remember how nice it was when there was someone there to heat them up for me, but I don't have anyone to do that, and I don't think I want anyone for the moment.

I hear faint murmurings coming from Julien and Gaëlle across the two closed doors. And then the rustling of covers. They must be making the most of a full night together. It doesn't really bother me though. Let them enjoy themselves.

I fall asleep, but at about two in the morning my eyes are wide open again. I move around in my bed, making as little noise as possible. The hospital visit turns over and over in my head, like clothes in a washing machine. Slowly the minutes pass, until eventually I hear Clara start to get restless. I go to the kitchen to heat the bottle and return with the nursing pillow. I don't know who invented those, but I can't imagine how anyone's arms survived feeding a baby before them.

I pick her up carefully before she starts crying properly and place her onto the cushion. I get back into bed, leaning back against the wall to be more comfortable. She puts her little mouth around the teat. The sucking noise lulls me gently. I put the bottle to the side when she has finished, and we fall asleep like that, with her lying peacefully in my arms.

5

Elsa

I wonder how long I'll only be able to hear for. I mean, I wonder if one day I'll wake up properly. I know, from what the doctors say, that I can't breathe very well on my own. When they do tests, I only hold out for a few hours before I'm too weak to breathe by myself. The mechanics of the body really are strange. But miraculous too. How is it possible that I can breathe, even for a few minutes, by myself, when I can't feel a thing? If I come out of the coma, that's another thing I must remember to ask about. My doctor won't know what's hit him. At the moment he pokes his head around the door every week or so, if I'm lucky. When I wake up he'll be bombarded.

Today is Saturday. My sister was here three days ago, it's only four more days until she comes again. Perhaps my parents will come today. After all, it was my birthday on Wednesday.

And it was a good day. I got to hear my friends – they hadn't been for a little while. I got to imagine them eating my cake, blowing out my candles and opening my present. And I made a new friend.

Thibault. I have managed to remember his name. It's strange, I was afraid I'd forget it. My memory doesn't seem at all affected by my vegetative state, but I was worried all the same. And, for the first time in six weeks, I haven't relived the accident in my dreams. In fact I haven't had any particular dreams at all. It's just been black and deep. Relaxing.

This morning, the care assistant came in to clean me and do my hair, as she does every morning. From the little splashes moving around me, I think she must have washed almost my entire body, and I heard her brushing my hair. I hope she hasn't given me a ridiculous hairstyle. They're mostly careful, I think, but looking after an inert body can't be an easy, or a graceful task. I don't know much about what she does, only that she's there. It's difficult to know what people are doing around me if they don't explain. I need points of reference and comparison for sounds. I have no memory of my mother doing my hair for me, so I can't really say what the care assistant was doing with it. On the other hand, I know that she forgot to put the lip balm on me because I didn't hear the lid of the pot, or the viscous sound of her rubbing it on. Twenty-four hours without lip balm is no big deal, and it's not as though I'll be having conversations with anyone, but I do still care about the state of my lips.

At work, I used to get through a whole pot in less than a month. Some people have their phones in their pockets at all times, or always take tissues or a plaster wherever they go; I always have my lip balm with me. If not my mouth would be like the texture of cardboard – not very pleasant.

Not very pleasant for who though? For me, I think. As far as I know, I don't keep my lips soft particularly for the benefit of any of the boys I've kissed, or might kiss in the future; it's just because it feels nicer. I love kissing, even though I can't do it now. I think the contact of lips on lips is a miracle. I never wear lipstick either, not even for special occasions. It's thicker than lip balm and I believe it dulls the senses.

Anyway, today the care assistant forgot my lip balm. Someone called her from the corridor, so she finished and left in a hurry. Since then, I've only heard the general bustling of an afternoon in the hospital. There are lots of visitors on Saturdays, but they're not visiting me.

Oh. I spoke too soon. I can hear the door handle. I recognise my mother's footsteps, and the heavier, more pronounced footsteps of my father. They are whispering to each other. I hate it. You'd think they had just stepped into a mortuary. I want to cry out that I'm still here, alive, right next to them, but they carry on talking in low voices as though they don't want me to hear them.

'. . . right to ask the question, Henry. It's been almost five months.'

'How can you talk like that?'

My father's belligerence is discernible even in his whispers.

'I'm trying to put myself in her place,' continues my mother. 'What would *I* think of all this? Would *I* want it to go on?'

'How can you put yourself in her place?'

'I'm trying! You're contradicting me for the sake of it!'

'I'm trying to weigh up the pros and cons. We're talking about ending the life of our daughter, not choosing the colour of our next carpet!'

If I could feel, I would have felt the blood run cold in my veins right then. First with surprise, because my father seems, more or less, to be defending me. But mainly because my parents are actually thinking about taking me off the life support.

'But maybe she'd go on breathing by herself,' tries my mother.

'It would be like every other time – in two hours she'd be on the verge of asphyxiating.'

'Maybe she doesn't want to go on fighting.'

'Stop thinking for her. You don't know anything about it,' says my father, angrily.

'Henry!'

'What?'

'Think about this, please!'

A moment passes in silence. I don't know if my father has replied with a gesture, or if he's still thinking.

'OK, I'll consider it. But not today.'

I deliberately remove myself for the rest of their conversation. I'm elsewhere. Rambling, almost delirious, alone with my thoughts. It's enough to make you lose your mind, spending all your time talking to yourself. But listening to other people talk about you introduces even more chaos.

I regain awareness of their presence when I hear them get up to leave. I need to stop doing that when people come here to see me, to speak to me. They must assume that I am at least trying to listen to them. That's how it is with my sister, anyway. And I only give her five minutes of attention – four at the start, and one at the end. But actually, who cares? They can't tell whether I'm paying attention or not.

My parents leave the room. I didn't even get a kiss, or if I did it was so perfunctory that I couldn't hear it.

I'm just preparing to be alone with myself again when I hear the door handle turn. My mother must have left her scarf or something. But it's not her walk, and it's not my father's either. It's lighter and somehow hesitant at the same time. It can't be my sister because she would have made herself known immediately. Perhaps it's the care assistant come to finish what she started this morning. Who knows, she might have remembered that she didn't do my lip balm.

'Hello, Elsa.'

The sound reaches my ears like a cool breeze. But the name rushes back into my mind with gale force. Thibault. He's come back. I don't know why. I want to believe that it's just because he felt like it. Who cares, he's here, and it makes a change even if he has only come to sleep.

'It still smells so much of jasmine in this room. Who puts it in here?'

The care assistant, I would like to answer, with the little vial of essential oil my mother gave her. Perhaps she's been a bit heavy-handed with it today.

'It doesn't matter, it smells good anyway.'

I hear him take off his jacket and even undo his shoelaces. He's making himself comfortable, which means that he's going to stay. I could jump for joy. Ha!

I hear the shoes being placed in a corner and the jacket on some piece of furniture at the back of the room. And a jumper or a sweatshirt too. It must be hot in my room. This is confirmed moments later.

'It's so hot in this room! I'm down to my T-shirt, I hope you don't mind. Don't worry, I'll stop undressing now, got to maintain some semblance of decency in here.'

I listen avidly to everything he says and does, even though I am having difficulty understanding his behaviour, his friendliness, his presence. Why has he come back?

'You must be asking yourself why I'm here. I've come with my mum to visit my brother. He's in room 55, you might remember. Though, I don't know why I expect you to remember anything. You almost certainly can't hear me, and I bet if I touch your arm you won't feel a thing. God, I'm talking to myself . . . what is wrong with me?'

I can understand his confusion, but I'd still like to give him a clip around the ear for assuming I'm not here, and then tell him to carry on speaking to me. Doesn't he know how important it is to speak to people in comas?

'I don't know anything about comas,' he begins suddenly. 'I've never known anyone who's been in a coma before, and I hope I never will in the future either. I've got a feeling it's good to talk though, so I will. But I don't have the faintest hope that you'll hear me. Which isn't necessarily a bad thing. Talking to you is like having a free session with a therapist, and you won't repeat a word I say. First, though, I'm going to open the window because it's absolutely boiling in here, and I usually feel the cold. I won't ask you if you mind – you can't tell me anyway.'

I'm pleasantly surprised. This is the first time anyone has spoken to me without condescension. Normally, people who come in here are pirouetting absurdly around me and bending over backwards to be polite, and considerate, as though I will suddenly be offended or ask them for something. Thibault is the first one to realise that since I am about as interactive as a grapefruit at the moment, there's really no point in bowing or curtseying when you're in my room.

I hear the window slide open and the air rush in. I imagine myself shivering.

'Brrrr! I'm not staying by this window either!' he exclaims. 'Over here will be just fine.' I hear a chair being dragged to the left side of my bed.

A smothered electric sound comes from across the room.

'Shit, I didn't turn my phone off. Excuse me, Elsa, I'd better take it. Even if you're probably going to go completely mad about it.'

I want to laugh. And then suddenly I want to cry. Or, rather, I wish my body was capable of crying. Not from sadness, but from joy. Thibault is also the first person to have made me want to laugh in six weeks. Even the rotten jokes of the DJ on the cleaning lady's radio haven't worked yet.

He's hardly picked up the phone when I hear him metamorphose into an ecology consultant.

'Slow down, what are you saying? No, absolutely not, that file hasn't been checked yet. I don't think their water system was passed . . . Yes, it's a wind power project, so the water system isn't important, but it's still the law . . . Are they trying to make you rush it through? Ah, they drive me mad, these people! They think we can rewrite the rules to suit them . . . OK . . . Listen, it's Saturday, calm down. The world is not going to come to an end between now and Monday, and if it does, frankly, no one will care about this wind project any more anyway – so just breathe. We can go through it together early on Monday morning if you like . . . See you at seven then? Yeah, you'll have to make it worth my while to get up at the crack of dawn though . . . Um, I don't know . . . A pineapple juice? . . . Yes, with pleasure!'

Thibault starts laughing. It's the most glorious sound I've ever heard. In my head, I start trying to draw the sound to see what it looks like. It reminds me of a flame flickering, or a pair of golden wings, flapping up and down with the sound of his voice. With each new burst of laughter, they flap away some of the blackness from around me, and everything lightens a little. When his laughter stops I hang on to the glow of those wings for as long as I can.

He speaks: 'Monday at seven it is!'

He hangs up and his fingers make a tapping sound on the phone for a moment.

'There, it's off. It won't disturb us again. Well, it won't disturb *me* again.'

I hear him put the phone into a pocket of his jacket and sit back down in the plastic chair.

'They're not very comfortable, are they, these chairs? They ought to put something a bit more upholstered in here. I don't suppose you care one way or another, but for the people who come to visit you it would be better. Maybe they'd stay a bit longer.'

That's not such a bad idea. But I doubt he'll get round to suggesting it to the hospital staff.

'I'm sure if you were sitting here you'd say the same. You can try it out one day, if you like. When you're back on your feet. I have no idea how I managed to fall asleep on this thing last time!'

He slides down the chair and puts his feet on my covers. A few moments later, he is breathing deeply. How does he get to sleep so quickly? What a marvellous talent – to fall asleep as soon as your head hits the pillow every night! Or maybe it's not like that, perhaps he doesn't sleep at night at all and that's why he makes up for it in the afternoons in people's hospital rooms.

I spend a long time listening to him breathe.

I listen to the wind, too. There must be a tree not far from my bedroom window. My sister described the colour of the autumn leaves to me once. Perhaps those same leaves are falling now. I'd love to be able to hear the noises on the ground and the conversations down below as well, but I'm on the fifth floor. I'd even love to hear the traffic, or the sound of car horns beeping, but everyone must know that it's illegal to beep your horn near a hospital.

I'm cold.

No. What am I saying? I can't be cold. I'm just *imagining* that I'm cold.

Maybe I fell asleep for a moment. I don't really know, because I can still hear the same thing: the wind and Thibault's steady breathing. I'd like him to wake up and make fun of me again.

A few moments later my wish is granted. I hear him stirring. An exasperated noise.

'Argh . . . this is about as comfortable as a kick up the arse.'

He must be rubbing his eyes and stretching as he takes his feet off the bed.

'Next time I'm bringing a cushion, Elsa!'

He's going to come back. If only I could scream aloud with joy.

'And next time, I won't open the window. You might not have noticed, but it's absolutely freezing in here now! I might have to put one of my layers back on just to go over and close it.'

The window slides shut. The wind stops making the leaves dance.

'My mother will be wondering where I've gone. And I told her to call me when she was ready. What an idiot!'

I hear him looking for his phone and then he must turn it back on. A message alert noise.

'Yep, she's waiting for me. She's only been there ten minutes, though. Phew! Well, I'd better go.'

He puts his shoes back on, his jacket, his gloves. I've put gloves on my hands so many times that I recognise the sound without even having to try. Thibault comes closer. I know what's coming next and I rejoice in anticipation.

'Come here and let me give you a kiss. In a manner of speaking.'

Like the first day, he moves my life support tubes out of the way. This kiss is a bit longer than the last one and, as far as I can make out, just about in the middle of my cheek. He's the only one who dares move all those tubes.

'Your cheeks are cold. Perhaps I shouldn't have opened the window. And look . . . those aren't lips you've got there! They're like bits of scrunched-up old newspaper. Is that what they pay them for, these nurses?'

He moves away and I hear the cupboard doors open and close.

'My brother's in there with lips like a Botoxed Hollywood actress and they leave you here like this! They've forgotten you because you're so quiet. That's not right. Anyone could need to kiss these lips.'

A crisp silence follows, as though someone has cut through the sound with a pair of scissors. But I can still hear the hustle and bustle outside in the corridor. I wonder why Thibault broke off so suddenly. Perhaps he found the pot of lip balm.

'We'll have to use mine.'

No, he didn't find it. And, strangely, his voice has changed. It sounds less chirpy, lower. Almost as though he's embarrassed.

'Here you go. That's better. I've never put lip balm on anyone before. I've never put lipstick on anyone either, my exes I mean, so it's extra strange to be doing this. But it's necessary. And if you don't like me doing it, you can't complain anyway.'

He puts the lid on with a little click.

'I'd better go. See you next time? Pff . . . you never answer. Maybe that's your way of telling me to leave you alone. That's not a bad idea actually. That way I won't have to go and explain to my best mate, when he asks, that I've been to see you again for absolutely no reason.'

He stops. I hear a sigh. I'll take that as goodbye. I imagine him smiling. If possible, with sincerity rather than sadness. The footsteps move away, the door handle squeaks, the door closes.

Let it be next week already.

6
Thibault

'Where were you?'

'Just around.'

'Oh.'

My mother lowers her head and looks at her shoes. She must know every detail of them off by heart, the amount of time she spends staring at them.

'What were you doing?' she continues after a moment.

'I was asleep.'

'Oh, good.'

'Yes.'

I don't want to lie, but I know this interrogation could go on for a little while, so I need to weigh each word and make sure I don't find myself having to reveal the whole bizarre truth.

'So you've found a place to sleep?' she says, surprised.

'A place, yes. Somewhere quiet.'

Awkward, but I still haven't lied. I even added a little extra detail, hoping that she would stop there, and she does.

She asks questions, my mother, but she also gives up easily. Perhaps with my brother's situation she's just reached a general state of resignation. I have no idea how she feels in fact, apart from the deep sadness that emanates from her every gesture and glance. I feel ashamed. She's in distress beside me and I haven't been doing anything to help, except sleeping on her sofa a few times a week. She hasn't been doing anything to help me either, but I think it would be selfish to expect her to worry about me at a time like this. So I make an effort.

'How are you getting on, Mum?'

My question surprises her, to the extent that she stops walking, even though we're now only a few paces from the car.

'Why are you asking me that?'

'It's about time I asked, isn't it? So, how are you?'

'Not good.'

'I guessed that. Come on – details, Mum.'

She looks at me as though there might be a catch. As though I'm eight years old and she knows that there's mischief behind the angelic grin.

'Well. Your brother might be an amateur murderer, but he's still also my son.'

This feels like a cold shower. Her tone is completely neutral. All this time I've been thinking that she was weak and didn't know how to handle her emotions. I think I have misjudged her. I forget that my mother is probably the strongest person I know, she just cries a little too easily.

'How do you reconcile the two?' I ask her.

'I love him, in exactly the same way that I love you.'

'Is that enough to forgive him?'

'It's not up to me to forgive him for anything . . .'

I know the next part by heart because I've already heard it a hundred times.

'. . . because it's not for you to judge,' I finish for her.

She nods her head.

'Neither you nor I owe anyone any judgement here. Your brother has already judged himself. And even though I spent your whole childhood telling you not to judge yourselves or anyone else, I have to admit that in this case I don't think it's a bad thing that he has all this time to reflect. I'm here for him if he needs me. I just wonder if I could have been more rigorous about educating him; perhaps I could have prevented him from getting behind that wheel a month ago.'

'Whatever education you gave us has worked on me.'

'But not on him,' she sighs.

'Don't blame yourself.'

'I don't blame myself. I'm sorry that the lives of two young girls have been stolen. I'm so sorry,' she swallows, 'but your brother is an adult. He is wrestling with his own conscience.'

She starts walking again and stops at the passenger door. I go over and unlock it. She stands there while I go round to the driver's side, her head over the roof.

'Why do you cry so much?' I ask, without looking at her.

'Because my son's life is ruined.'

'That's his fault!' I say, immediately.

'Sure, but he's still not OK, and it's my job as his mother to be there for him.'

'So you'll go on visiting him like this until his trial, and then you'll carry on visiting him when he's in prison?'

I feel the anger rising in me again, my tone becoming more and more aggressive.

'Yes,' she murmurs.

She opens the door and gets into the car. I'm still outside, my hand on the handle. I take a deep breath to calm myself down and get into the car as well.

'You'll understand when you have children of your own,' she tells me when I'm sitting down.

'Well for now, I don't.'

'For now . . .' she repeats.

The conversation stops there. I'm on edge. But there is one good thing: for the first time in weeks my mother isn't crying. I think our conversation has shaken her. It has certainly shaken me.

I drop her at her apartment fifteen minutes later, explaining that I'm going to spend a few nights at my place. She accepts this without showing any emotion. I feel as though I've driven home an empty shell. I think I almost preferred it when she was weeping at me.

I arrive back at mine, frozen to the bone. My car heater is erratic at the best of times, but today it's been on strike. I stand under an almost boiling shower to get myself back to room temperature and come out pink all over. In the mirror my hair still looks a mess, but I know it would be a waste of time trying to tame it.

I pick up the razor and attack my three-day mini-beard. I wouldn't normally do this on a Saturday. I'd wait until Monday morning before work, but I'm in the mood for a shave.

It keeps my hands occupied while my mind whizzes all over the place. And as soon as I've finished shaving I set to cleaning my apartment.

I think again about what my mother said. *You'll understand when you have children of your own.* Amid all these uncertainties, that's the only thing I'm sure about at the moment. I do want children one day. Little Clara has convinced me beyond all doubt of that.

When I stayed at Julien's the other night, and fell asleep with her in my arms, it was Gaëlle who eventually came in to wake us up at about eight the next morning. She even took a photo – I've got it on my phone. I'll treasure it and show it to Clara when she's older, her crazy, doting godfather holding her in his arms when she was only a few months old.

I'm hoovering so I don't hear the doorbell ring straight away. It's only when I turn off the blaring noise, like the sound of a plane's engine, that I notice that someone is persistently pressing the button. I pull on a T-shirt and just avoid tripping over the electric wire of the vacuum cleaner, still trailing across the hallway.

'Hi . . . Cindy?'

My ex is standing in front of me when I open the door. Her blonde hair is still impeccable, exactly as it always was, her hourglass figure is even more voluptuously contoured than in my memory. I'm speechless, my mouth is half open, my hand unmoving on the latch.

'Hello, Thibault,' she replies. 'Can I come in?'

I stutter like an imbecile and in the end, I just move out of the way, motioning towards the living room. Cindy walks past me in the doorway and kisses me on the cheek. I close the door, still dumbfounded. When I turn round, she is taking off her coat and high-heeled shoes. I recognise the black stockings and the skirt she is wearing. The blouse is new; it suits her.

She sees me looking and smiles. I come back to my senses and go and put on some trousers.

'What are you doing?' she asks.

'Getting dressed,' I call from my bedroom.

'You were already dressed,' she says.

'Not for visitors.'

'It's only me. I've seen you naked, I think I can manage a pair of shorts.'

I know she's right, but I still prefer to be wearing trousers. I find a pair of baggy jeans on the chair and hurriedly pull them on. When I come back into the living room, Cindy is sitting on the sofa rubbing her feet.

'Those heels were killing me!' she groans.

'I've never understood why women wear those.'

'Because it gives a better line, Thibault. Don't you think?'

'I . . .'

'You used to like it, when I . . .'

She doesn't finish her sentence. She doesn't need to. We both know what she's trying to say. My good upbringing saves me, propelling me into the kitchen.

'Would you like something to drink?'

'I'd love a glass of wine, if you've got any.'

'I might, at the back of a cupboard, but I'm not making any promises.'

'Ah yes, I remember, Mister Fruit Juice,' she says, laughing.

I rummage in the cupboards and eventually find a bottle. In fact I think it dates back to the breakup, when my brother came over and tried to cheer me up with an impromptu party. I come back with two full glasses. One of wine, the other of pineapple juice.

'What are you drinking?' she asks.

'Same as usual.'

'Ah.'

I wonder if she even remembers what I used to drink. We were together for a long time, but she always seemed to stay pretty casual, nonchalant even, about her feelings for me. I didn't mind at the time but thinking about it now, there was something insincere about it. I thought I knew the minutest detail of everything about her, but she wasn't interested in anything much about me, beyond the essentials.

'So . . . Why are you here?' I ask, when I've given her the wine.

'You don't waste any time!' she exclaims, taking a sip.

'Well you have to admit, this is a bit unexpected.'

'You're right. But I've just come to catch up.'

The Book in my head immediately flips open. If Cindy wants to come over and catch up, go to page 15. I get to page 15 and it says: Warning!

'Oh,' I say, flatly. 'Well, as can you see, nothing's changed.'

Or almost nothing, I say to myself. I have no intention of telling her anything about the past few days – or weeks.

'How's Julien?' she asks. 'Has Gaëlle had the baby?'

'Yes, she's wonderful.'

'Gaëlle or the baby?'

'Both.'

She takes another sip of wine and puts her glass down. My phone is on the table beside me.

'Here, I've got a picture, if you'd like to see her,' I say, picking it up.

I was expecting to pass her the phone, but Cindy comes over and sits next to me. I scroll through the photos until I get to the one of Clara and me asleep. She looks at it for a long time without saying anything, and then she looks at me.

'Very sweet. How long ago was that?'

'Only a few days.'

'You stayed the night there?'

I lower my head. I get the feeling she also has her own version of *The Book in Which I Am the Hero* open in her head. Mine is resting open at page 80: Just Be Polite.

'And you?' I say, to avoid an uncomfortable silence. 'What's new?'

'Oh, you know, work, different department, but I like it.'

'Which area are you in now?'

'South west.'

'Oh, quite a way from here!'

'Yes, but I still come back and forth quite a lot. Like this weekend. To see family and friends.'

'Am I one of the friends?'

I've just made a little departure from page 80, veering towards: Wind Her up a Bit. But she doesn't seem bothered by my question.

'Of course!' she exclaims.

'Hmm . . .'

'Why? Am I not *your* friend?'

That sounds like the million-dollar question. Page 77: Be Sincere.

'I don't think it's quite accurate to say that we're friends, no, given our history and the way it ended.'

'Are you still upset with me?'

Honestly, I don't know how I feel, but I'm not in the mood to start diving into explanations.

'No, it's fine.'

'So why can't you consider me a friend?'

She fixes me with her big eyes. Her makeup makes them stand out, wider than ever. I can smell her perfume. It's still the same one, if I remember rightly, and I ought to recognise the fragrance I lived with for years. I shuffle to get further away from her. When did she move so close?

'So, Thibault, tell me, why?'

Her voice is a whisper. I can feel her breathing and behind the perfume I can smell her skin. Memories confuse themselves in my head and I want to drive them away. But at the same time . . .

'I . . . I don't know. It's tricky?'

Ridiculous response, but it's all I can come up with.

Cindy stares at me intently and I remember in a flash all the other times she has looked at me that way. I see the same memories in her head too. Her *Book* gives her a quicker solution than mine does me. The next moment she is kissing me, and I am responding almost without thought.

Almost. Part of me is desperate for the contact. Another part of me is sickened by it.

I feel Cindy take my hand and put it around her waist while she lets her own hand wander up and down my back. She draws me towards her and I stretch myself out along the sofa.

'Interesting,' she murmurs. 'I didn't know you liked being on the bottom.'

'There are lots of things you didn't know about me,' I reply coldly.

I see in her eyes that she is surprised by my tone but I force myself to continue, before desire carries me away again.

'What are you doing here, Cindy?'

She freezes. Her *Book* clearly doesn't have a response for that.

'No,' I continue, 'I don't actually need a reply. I've got enough of an idea and, honestly, I'm not that interested anyway.'

I get up, leaving her lying on the sofa. The look on her face has changed completely. She is looking at me like I'm something the cat dragged in. I don't blame her, I would probably look the same.

'Get out,' I say.

She doesn't utter a word, but begins to gather her stuff. I watch her putting on her shoes, re-buttoning her shirt right to the top (when had she undone it?). I hand over her coat and open the door before she has even put it on.

'You've changed,' she says to me as she steps over the threshold.

'If you had ever bothered to get to know me in the first place, you could have saved yourself the trouble of coming.'

'I would still at least have tried—'

I close the door without saying anything else.

I forgot about 'Just Be Polite' a few minutes ago.

On the table is her half-finished glass of wine and my juice, untouched. I pick up the glass, go into the kitchen and pour it down the sink, along with the rest of the bottle. I put the whole lot into my recycling bin; I don't want to see that glass again.

When I go back into the living room I don't even dare look at the sofa. I go and get a blanket from my bedroom and throw it over the top. Better already. I pick up the remote control and switch on the TV, sipping my drink without really paying attention to what the presenter is saying.

That was mortifying.

No wonder I'm not looking for anyone else.

7
Elsa

It's Monday. I won't have any visitors today. The days without visits have come to seem interminable, especially since Thibault entered my semblance of a life. With any luck, he might come and visit his brother, or rather bring his mother to visit his brother. But, on a weekday, perhaps he probably won't have the time.

I listen to the care assistant going through her routine. This time she doesn't forget a thing. It seems to go on for too long, in fact! You'd think she was preparing me for a ceremony or something. She's really paying attention to my lips, as though she's trying to make up for forgetting them before.

She finishes without speaking to me, as always, and then leaves the room. A few minutes later, the door opens noisily and a chorus of voices and clattering footsteps enters my room. I am taken aback by the volume. Why so many people?

I catch a few medical terms in the midst of all the kerfuffle, but when there is so much going on at once, it's difficult to follow. I've developed quite a talent (in a manner of speaking) for identifying the head doctor among his group of juniors. It must be this doctor, the consultant, who has just clapped his hands, because the noise subsides and gradually everyone falls silent.

As far as I can tell from their breathing, I am surrounded by about five junior doctors, or 'house officers' as they seem to call each other. I have become a teaching aid! The consultant, standing at the foot of my bed, picks up the clipboard, which has my 'system updates', as I like to think of them, written on it. It's been a while since anyone wrote anything on there.

'Right everyone, the case of room 52,' the doctor begins. 'Multiple traumas, including to the head. Deep coma for almost five months. I'll leave you to read the details.'

Great, I'm a number now, as well as a 'case' . . .

The clipboard is passed from hand to hand, not staying with any one person for longer than a couple of seconds. There must be a rule amongst doctors about never keeping a single page in front of their eyes for too long. Maybe they get bored of reading these clipboards again and again, or maybe they just prefer to judge for themselves. Or perhaps it is part of their training to assess all the essentials of any medical situation within five seconds. Yes, that must be it, they are just practising what they've been trained to do. All the same, I'd love it if there were one doctor who invested more than five seconds in the case of room 52. They might discover that I can hear everything they are saying.

'Here's a copy of the brain imaging. All the common features, of course. I've included details of her state on arrival in July, and also the one from two months ago. I await your comments.'

This time, it takes a little longer than five seconds. I hear them whispering but I don't catch any of the details. It's far too technical for me anyway, but I can sense that they are most concerned with impressing the consultant. They seem to be conducting quite an in-depth evaluation.

'So,' begins the consultant. 'What do we think?'

One of the juniors on my right speaks first.

'Her imaging has improved from July to November?'

'More or less, but I would have liked some more details. You need to justify why it is you think that. In fact, you can all leave your thoughts written up on my desk tomorrow morning. Swot up on it tonight.'

I hear some murmurs of protestation, but they die down quickly.

'What else?' the doctor goes on.

'Sir?' says another trainee.

'Yes, Fabrice.'

'Can we speak sincerely?'

'We can *only* speak with sincerity here. Even if it's not always the truth.'

'Can we also avoid dressing up the situation?' asks this junior named Fabrice.

'Between ourselves, yes,' replies the doctor. 'In the presence of relatives, it's not always advisable. Adapt your speech to the people in front of you. But please go on, we're listening.'

'Uh . . . well she's completely fucked, isn't she?'

I hear some sniggers, but the laughter is quickly curtailed.

'You really aren't dressing it up, are you, Fabrice?' says the doctor. 'But you're quite right. According to all the information that's in front of you, the reports of the different doctors who have examined her, and the absence of any marked improvement over the past three months, this patient just scrapes a two per cent probability of recovery.'

'Only two per cent?' asks the first junior doctor.

'Assuming, hypothetically, that she does wake up, we can't be sure how far the head trauma will have affected her mental and physical functions. Looking at the affected areas of the brain, we can predict that there may be complications with language and with fine motor skills on the right side. There is also likely to be other sensory and neurological impairment, and we know that her respiratory function, which has already been tested, is . . .'

I try desperately to move my attention away from what the doctor is saying and think about something else. I don't want to hear another word. Hearing seems to be the only thing that my body *can* still do and for the first time, I wish it couldn't.

I scroll through any other thoughts I might be able to bring to mind. The only one that calms me down is Thibault. I hardly know anything about him so I don't have a very detailed picture. But I let my mind wander and invent for a moment until the doctor's voice brings me back to what they are saying.

'. . . so, two per cent.'

'That's almost zero, really, isn't it?' says a trainee doctor I haven't heard speak before.

'Almost, yes. But we are scientists and we don't deal in *almost*.'

'So, that means . . .' the trainee starts.

'. . . it's zero,' finishes the consultant.

A trolley falls over in the corridor with an almighty crash, as if to reflect my state of mind. The house officers are scribbling notes. The doctor must be pleased with himself. He can move onto something else now the case study of room 52 is finished. But apparently it's not quite finished . . .

'What's the next stage?' he asks.

'Let the family know?' suggests the first junior.

'Exactly. I broached the matter with them a few days ago, so that they could start thinking about it.'

'What did they say? If it's OK to ask . . .'

'They said that they would think about it. The mother was resigned, the father was against, which is often the case. It's very unusual for relatives to agree. It's almost a natural state of contradiction. We don't talk lightly of ending the life support of a person who is in a coma.'

I don't like the way the doctor is speaking about my parents, but I have to admit that he's right.

'Isn't that what we've just been doing?' asks the first junior doctor suddenly.

My ears prick up. This comment must have surprised even the consultant, because he doesn't reply straight away.

'Can you explain yourself, Loris?' he says, in a voice which is trying to be neutral, but which comes out as abrupt.

'The terms that we have just been using, the "scientific" approximations that we've been making about the probability of her recovery. You say that we never speak lightly of ending the life support of a patient in a coma, but I think I just heard Fabrice say she was *completely fucked* and I'm pretty sure I also heard the conversion of a two per cent chance to zero. If that's not speaking lightly then I don't think we're talking the same language.'

If I could move, I would kiss this lovely house officer. But I think I might have to step in and physically defend him first because, given the tone of the consultant, Loris is going to be working night shifts for some time.

'Are you questioning the diagnostic abilities of your classmates and future colleagues?'

'I'm not questioning anything, sir,' returns Loris. 'I just find it strange to be so crude about someone who, as far as we can see, is still breathing here in front of us.'

'Loris,' begins the consultant, as though he is trying to collect himself, 'if you can't bear the idea that we might have to disconnect someone, you have no place in this department.'

'It has nothing to do with being able to bear it or not, sir. It has to do with facts. You say two per cent. For me, that means two per cent. It's not zero. As long as we haven't reached zero, I believe that there is still hope.'

'You're not here to hope, Loris.'

'What am I here for then?' replies the junior doctor, now purposefully insolent.

'To conclude that this case is closed. Resolved. Finished. It is going to be impossible to bring this patient back to consciousness. As your colleague said, she is fucked. And it matters very little to me if that term doesn't suit your delicate sensibilities.'

I think poor Loris might be on night shifts for the rest of his time in this training post.

My room falls silent. I imagine Loris holding the gaze of his teacher for a moment, and then lowering his eyes. I imagine all the other house officers feigning an urgent need to write something down. At least the session is over, and at least I wasn't able to see the expressions on their faces during the discussion – it could be devastating to witness this sort of situation when it concerns you. In any case, my only hope is to go on believing that they've got it wrong.

'Right then, Loris, since you seem to be so attached to this patient, you can write down the conclusions of our visit yourself.'

I hear my 'system updates' being passed over to my right. A few pencil scratchings later, and the clipboard is handed back to the doctor.

'Hmm . . . Well summarised, Loris. If you weren't so obstinate, I would almost certainly have you on my team when you qualify. You have, nevertheless, left out one detail.'

'What?'

The junior doctor doesn't seem as talkative now, and I can understand why. This consultant is really beginning to make my ears hurt.

'On the first page, you can add it underneath.'

'What has he left out?' asks another junior, as Loris begins to write.

'Can you answer your colleague?'

I can visualise perfectly the clenched fists and set jaw of poor Loris who has done nothing but stick up for me since he came into the room. But I have no idea what is being added to the first page of my file.

'I left out the official declaration of our intention to disconnect the life support of this patient. I'm just writing that we are now awaiting family agreement before we set the date.'

8

Thibault

I feel good today. Even if I did have to get up early. I helped my colleague sort out a wind power situation and I earned a pineapple juice in recompense. It was a rewarding start to the day, but I think I've had a good feeling about today ever since I woke up.

When, halfway through the morning, I realise why this is, I almost want to laugh out loud.

It's Monday and I'm meant to take my mother to the hospital this evening. It's the first time that I have ever contemplated this ordeal with a smile.

'Thibault? What is that dazed, idiotic expression on your face?'

My reflections are brought to an abrupt close when I see the colleague I helped out this morning standing, quizzical, in front of me. He is looking at me with his head tilted to one side, as though he is trying to read something on my chin. I, too, am quite curious to see what response I'll come up with.

'What are you talking about?' I say.

Disappointing.

'That smile, there,' he answers, pointing to the corner of my mouth. 'You've got a sort of smiley twitch.'

'You're smiling too!' I defend myself.

'That's because I'm amazed,' he laughs. 'Why this weird happy face? It's not like you at all, Thibault . . .'

'Mind your own business.'

'Oh, I see. Translation: it's a girl.'

'I said, mind your own business!'

'Translation: yes, it's definitely a girl! Hey, everyone, Thibault's got a new—'

He doesn't continue because I grab him by the shoulder and put my other hand over his mouth. My attempt is pathetic and he laughs noisily through my fingers. He understands, though, that I don't want him to spread it any further and quietens down.

'It's a lot more complicated than that,' I say, taking my useless hand away.

'OK,' he replies, still smiling. 'You let us know when you understand it better!' He walks away with a wink and I plunge back into my thoughts.

It really is a lot more complicated than that. I'm sitting here rejoicing at the thought of going to intensive care to visit a girl I don't know, who's in a profound coma.

Throughout the day my mind wanders from work to various other things, which always bring me back to Elsa. Sometimes they also bring me back to my brother. When five o'clock comes, I'm ready to race out of the door.

I go via my mother's to pick her up. She seems better. I park in the hospital car park and we get out of the car together. Presumably I still have my idiotic smile.

'What's happened to you, Thibault? You seem happy today.'

'Nothing special.'

Unlike my colleague, she is immediately satisfied with this response. I agree to take the lift with her, rather than the stairs, and we come out into the fifth-floor corridor together.

'Do you want to come in?' my mother attempts.

'No.'

'What are you going to do while you're waiting?'

'Just sleep. Maybe talk.'

'Who do you talk to?' she asks, surprised.

'To the wall,' I reply in a whisper.

We stop just in front of room 55. I watch my mother slip into the room. I glance briefly at my brother's bed. The covers are strewn with all sorts of things – paper, magazines, remote controls. Judging by the noise coming from the room, I assume that the television is on. I hesitate for half a second, and then let the door swing shut.

I'm not ready yet. I turn and go back towards room 52, half opening the door and poking my head around it. Perfect, there's no one there. I close it carefully behind me, as though worried I'll wake the person in the bed. It's funny, I still can't quite work out how I'm meant to behave around her.

I've only taken three steps in when I know that something has changed. I can sense a difference, and not a reassuring one. Half of the room is far too clean, and yet there are footprints all over the floor. The jasmine is masked by lots of other smells and, when I go over to the bed, I can see little bits of pencil eraser on the sheets.

People have been in here today. It's strange. It could be Elsa's family, but that would be surprising. Perhaps friends is more likely. That would explain all the footprints. On the other hand I don't know what they would have been drawing, and then rubbing out. But I leave all this aside and concentrate on Elsa. Or rather I concentrate on 'Elsa and me'.

Since this morning, I've felt almost euphoric at the thought of coming into this hospital room. It's not normal.

I keep repeating that over and over. It's not normal. It's not normal. There's nothing normal about getting excited over visiting someone who doesn't move, doesn't feel, doesn't think and doesn't speak, and who, above all, I do not actually know.

For the nth time since I first stumbled into this room, I wonder what I am doing here. And for the nth time I don't have the answer. It doesn't matter, I think to myself, *sometimes it's OK to be ignorant.* That's what my boss always says, but then he always ends with, *as long as we take steps to banish our ignorance as soon as we notice it's there.* Well, I'm long past that stage now. Perhaps I should be setting myself some kind of time limit, though – to force myself to figure out what I'm doing here and what I think it's going to achieve.

I go to a chair that is positioned at an angle to the bed. It's in its usual position, so presumably everyone must have stayed standing when they came in earlier. I don't go near the clipboard. From what I learned on my first visit, the doctors don't give much away on those pieces of paper. And from what I can make out in front of me, the wires, tubing and other apparatus that keep Elsa with us here on earth have neither increased nor diminished in number since I last saw them.

It's as though nothing has changed at all since I was last here.

Perhaps that's why I like it.

And all at once it seems so obvious that I sigh out loud. Of course, that's why I come here! Nothing changes in this room. Elsa is always here, passive, immobile. She always breathes with the same rhythm. Things are always left in the same place – well, what few things there are. Only the main chair navigates a few centimetres this way or that, but otherwise it's like a bubble in which time has stopped.

It's a bubble to which I have temporary access. How long will I stay in this bubble? How long will Elsa stay in this bubble?

I sit down. Great, I've just found the answer to one question and replaced it with two others! It looks as though my mind is always going to go round in circles whenever I'm in here.

I start thinking: it's Monday, maybe I'll give myself one more week. I can have until next Monday to consider what to do about these visits – surely that should be enough. It's not as though I have a hundred and one choices. Either I keep coming, or I stop coming. And as far as Elsa's concerned, either she stays asleep, or she wakes up. There's no way I can find a solution to Elsa's predicament, of course, but I can find a solution to mine. Today, though, I decide on a reprieve. I'll stop asking myself questions.

I've already taken off my shoes and my jacket, which makes me look like some sort of astronaut. I put away my gloves, my scarf, my papers, the car keys, the keys to my mother's house and to mine. I seem to have most of the contents of my apartment with me, in fact. Not that there's much there. I didn't keep anything that I'd shared with Cindy, so that meant getting rid of lots of my things, both useless and useful. My mother says that I should make the new place more my own, but she also says many other things that I ignore, so I haven't done anything about it yet.

I install myself in the chair. At least I try to, groaning aloud when I realise that I have forgotten to bring a cushion with me to make the rigid plastic a bit more comfortable. I consider my jacket, but it won't help much as a cushion. I look around as though I might find a solution somewhere else in the room. I can't see anything. I check the little shower room in case there's something in there – but there isn't, not so much as a towel or even a comb or a toothbrush to serve as my cushion. I come back into the bedroom and see my only possibility. And then I realise that I've been incredibly rude ever since my entrance.

'Shit! Uh . . . sorry, Elsa. Hello. I was in another world – I was thinking. Yes, it does happen from time to time . . . There's too much going round and round in my head at the moment to give you a brief summary of my thoughts, so I'll leave it at that for now. Let's be honest, it's not as if you're going to talk it all through with me anyway.'

I look around once more. I don't really like the solution

I've found, but it's better than nothing, and who will ever know? The only person who could actually be bothered by it probably won't even realise.

I go over to the bed and run my hands over the wires. When my fingers hover over the pillow, my muscles stiffen involuntarily. I can't. First, because an inanimate body is very heavy. Even though Elsa can't weigh more than about fifty kilos, she would still be a significant weight to lift. And second, because I don't want to make her feel uncomfortable, even though she probably wouldn't feel a thing. It would be as though I were taking advantage. I wouldn't be comfortable with that either.

I stay still for several seconds, and then I take my hands away and put the wires, tubing and other things carefully back in place. Elsa hasn't moved a muscle; though I'm not sure what I was expecting from her.

'Do you remember when I said the chair was uncomfortable?' I say, returning to the object in question. 'Well, I was thinking about borrowing one of your pillows, but you look pretty well settled there, so it wouldn't have been very gentlemanly of me. Never mind for now! I'll just sit it out on this hard chair that's like a plank of wood, all rigid and unmoving, while you stay comfortable under your nice soft covers. And before you protest, I mean it: you don't need to worry about me, Elsa. But thanks anyway.'

After ten minutes, I am more than certain that this chair is an instrument of torture, conceived to keep visitors from staying too long. The doctors and nurses don't like it when there are too many people in the rooms. With this type of furniture they can rest assured that no one will ever linger. I wriggle around on the plastic, seriously thinking of leaving. I could just go and freeze in the car while I wait for my mother.

But I don't want to leave.

The Book comes open in my head and then takes me to page 13, which says: 'There Is Only One Option Available to You'.

Yes, I know what that is, but it's not exactly the best idea I've had. In fact it's downright inappropriate, and if anyone came into the room I wouldn't be able to get away with my 'I'm just a friend' line.

I sigh for the fortieth time since I arrived, and get up again. I feel like a child who is about to own up to doing something naughty. Except in this case, I'm pre-emptively owning up before it actually happens.

'So, Elsa. I'm afraid this chair really isn't working for me after all. Either I can go . . . or you can make a bit of room for me on there.'

I've already started making my way around the bed to install myself by the window. It looks as though there's a bit more space on that side, but it's only an illusion because actually she's positioned right in the centre, so that the mattress fits snugly around the indent made by her body. I move towards that side, so that I'll have a little protection if anyone comes into the room. With a bit of luck no one will be able to see me at all once I'm lying down. With a lot of luck, no one will even come past.

I slide my hands underneath Elsa, careful to pick up the blanket as well. I can't bring myself to put my hands directly on the gown covering her frail body. I try to lift her and move her over a little bit, without disturbing the wires or anything else. I fail.

Letting out my forty-first sigh since coming into the room, I pick up the clipboard at the foot of the bed. She weighed fifty-four kilos when she arrived at the hospital. In her state she could easily have lost six, if not more. Good grief, I'm not even capable of lifting forty-eight kilos. I'm going to have to do some sport.

I forget the idea of moving Elsa and content myself with moving all the wires to the other side. I lie down silently beside her, ramrod straight in the thirty centimetres of mattress available to me, but oddly enough I relax immediately.

The mattress is strange. It doesn't feel anything like my bed at home, but I suppose if a person's got to lie, or half sit on this thing for weeks on end, there must be a material adapted specifically to suit their requirements.

Reassured, I position myself again, with my back to Elsa. In spite of her inactivity, her warm body has the effect of a cover.

Very comfortable, these mattresses . . .

I'm asleep in less than ten seconds.

directly on the gown covering her frail body. I try to lift her and move her over a little bit, without disturbing the wires or anything else. I fail.

Letting out my forty-first sigh since coming into the room, I pick up the clipboard at the foot of the bed. She weighed fifty-four kilos when she arrived at the hospital. In her state she could easily have lost six. That makes... Good grief, I'm not even capable of lifting forty-eight kilos. I'm going to have to do some sport.

I forget the idea of moving Elsa and content myself with moving all the wires to the other side. I lie down silently beside her, pinned straight in the thirty centimetres of mattress available to me, but oddly enough I relax immediately.

The mattress is strange. It doesn't feel anything like my bed at home, but I suppose if a person's got to lie, or half sit on this thing for weeks on end, there must be a material adapted specifically to suit their requirements.

Reassured, I position myself again, with my back to Elsa. In spite of her inactivity, her warm body has the effect of a cover.

Very comfortable, these mattresses ...

I'm asleep in less than ten seconds.

9

Elsa

Even if I could move, I don't think I would want to. I'd stay absolutely still so as not to disturb him, and silent so as not to wake him up. Perhaps I would let myself turn my head a little to watch him sleep, but nothing more.

I followed all of Thibault's to-ings and fro-ings about what to do before he lay down with a new kind of heightened attention. I never dreamt that he was going to lie down next to me. I'd have thought it might feel a bit morbid to try and go to sleep on the same bed as a person in a coma but, once again, my visitor surprises me. And to think that my mother sometimes hardly dares to touch me. Thibault is practically glued to my side. At least I think he is. I have to assume my bed is not enormous, so there must certainly be parts of us that are in contact with each other.

Physical contact . . . the thought makes me want to quiver with delight, or jump up and down like a little girl at the prospect of chocolate ice cream. I haven't felt the slightest tactile sensation in almost twenty-one weeks. The last thing I felt was the snow covering my body, which was not a wonderful feeling. In fact, I'd give my entire collection of climbing carabiners to feel even a patch of Thibault against me. There must be layers of clothes and covers between us, but some of his heat would transmit through to my skin and that would be enough.

To tell the truth, right now I could enjoy the idea of feeling contact with anyone at all – the care assistant coming to do my lip balm; my sister putting her hand on mine; Steve, Alex and Rebecca kissing my forehead. But Thibault is different. He's my secret. He's my breath of fresh air. Even though I still don't have a clue what he looks like.

Automatically, I ask my brain to turn my head and open my eyes, but then I realise the futility of this command: 'Tell my neurons to put my eyes back into operation.' Just like that. It won't work. They said so this morning.

I begin to wonder if I am actually capable of experiencing a feeling of hatred for those doctors, perhaps for all doctors and all their trainees, even the one who tried to stick up for me. They'll convince him to give up on me too, eventually. In my angry delirium, I see them all trooping across my imagination as evil villains in mint green scrubs with caricature heads. I start to hope that one of them makes a wrong diagnosis and gets the sack for it, but I stop myself.

No, a wrong diagnosis would mean that someone doesn't get cured. I can't wish that on anyone. Especially as that person could be me. It could easily be me . . .

It could be me!

I imagine myself leaping out of the bed, shouting something like 'Eureka!', but instead I internally congratulate myself.

It could be me, the wrong diagnosis, with all those theories I didn't understand about the remaining two per cent of hope.

My morale lifts with a single jolt. I feel like a seesaw.

That could be me. I could wake up and prove them wrong. After all, no one imagined that I'd be able to hear again, but it's happening already. If I could just open my eyes or give any outward sign of life . . .

The question remains, though: how to do it? At the moment all I do is listen and wait. But have I really tried to do anything else?

Five minutes ago, I chickened out of an attempt to turn my head because I thought I couldn't do it. I didn't see the point. They are all so categorical about me and what I'm capable of, but no one has actually experienced being in this coma . . . I am going to allow myself to doubt their theories. This is liberating.

A part of me also has to admit that the doctor made me angry. Even if only to annoy him, I'd like to be able to wake myself up. But today, here, I have a feeling there's another reason I'd like to wake up. And until now, I'd never really made the conscious effort to do it. It hadn't even crossed my mind, even though I have absolutely nothing to do but think.

Of course, the effort implies a general control of muscles, not to mention much more of the brain than is at my disposal at the moment. I don't control either one or the other, with the exception of the auditory zone, but if that section has agreed to start functioning again, why shouldn't the others follow? The big question remains, though: how am I going to teach myself?

The answer follows, as though it has been waiting for this moment to come forward. I have to think, of course, because at the moment it's the only thing I am capable of doing. To think that I am about to turn my head. To think that I am about to open my eyes and get my eyesight working. To imagine myself as powerful, a thinking superhero, capable of anything I set my mind to.

I brace myself for the onslaught.

Knowing that I have a hidden objective helps considerably. Well, it's not that hidden any more. I am dying to look at Thibault. If I manage to turn my head, which would already be quite a feat, and then to open my eyes, an achievement of miraculous proportions, I might at last be able to see what my favourite visitor looks like.

I should be blushing at these thoughts, but my parents aren't exactly great company on their visits and my sister's only interested in her boyfriends. And Steve, Alex and Rebecca don't come that often. There aren't many contenders for the top spot.

I spend the entire length of Thibault's nap commanding myself to turn my head and open my eyes. I alternate between the two because, frankly, the whole operation is rather tiresome, but I have the breathing of my temporary roommate beside me for motivation. Each time he breathes in, I imagine that I turn my head, each time he breathes out, I imagine that I open my eyes and see him. Every version of him that I imagine for myself is slightly different, but there are certain points which always stay the same. I am certain, for example, that he has brown hair, though I have no idea why.

I continue my mental efforts until I hear a movement on my right. The sound suggests that Thibault is not just stirring in his sleep, but waking up properly. He must have been snoozing for at least an hour while I've been trying to turn my head. And while he certainly succeeded at being asleep, I can't say as much for the success of my own new activity. Maybe the new thinking technique will have a cumulative power, but at the moment I don't feel the slightest change.

The grunting and sighing sounds next to me pull me from my reflections. He seems to sit up, then get up, and then he stops moving. I am starting to wonder why he is staying so still when the regular breathing I hear a little way from me stops suddenly.

'Shit! Your tubes!'

His exclamation gives me a shock. I wonder what the problem is with my tubes.

'I must have pushed you while I was asleep and it's pulled all of these gadgets. Luckily none of them have come out!'

Hearing him mutter like this is quite amusing, but I don't remember him moving enough to cause what he has just said has happened. I hear him rearrange my wiring. I often wonder what I must look like amid all these 'gadgets', as he describes them. I used to think I must look something like an insect in the middle of a spider's web. Then I decided that I preferred to think of myself as a carabiner in the middle of a rope rescue system. Like the ones they use to pull people out of crevasses. It's a bit more like me, and it certainly seems more sophisticated. But above all, it carries with it the notion of lifesaving. Whereas in the other case . . .

There's movement around me again when the door to my room opens. Thibault must freeze like a block of ice because I don't hear anything from his side. The new intruder comes in and Thibault still says nothing.

'Hello. Are you family?'

I recognise the voice of Loris, the junior doctor who defended me this morning. Now I know who he is, I wonder what he's doing here, but Thibault's answer interests me even more.

'No, I'm just a friend. And you? I mean . . . are you her doctor?'

I interpret the short silence as a head being shaken.

'I'm just a house officer doing the rounds.'

'Ah.'

I'd have given the same response as Thibault. In almost seven weeks, not a single 'house officer' has come to do any rounds. I think the session this morning has brought him here.

'Did you have a question?' he asks.

'Uh . . . no, nothing in particular.'

I hear Thibault move around the bed. He must be trying to collect his things and make a quick exit. When Steve, Alex and Rebecca surprised him, they managed to put him at ease, but today I have little hope that the junior doctor will be able to do the same because he's not saying a thing.

I try to picture the situation for myself. I remember that Thibault is still in his socks and that the covers on the right side of my bed must be messed up. I'd love to be able to laugh or to feel that little shiver of excitement I would surely experience at the prospect of his illicit imprint on the mattress being discovered. Just to feel the adrenaline of the forbidden, or at least the unexpected, would be quite exquisite.

I assume that Loris has noticed these details because he remains mute. Thibault gathers together his clothes and shoes clumsily. It must make him nervous to have someone watching him.

Finally I hear him come over to the bed and lean over me. I'm surprised that he dares to kiss my cheek in front of the doctor. But this movement is interrupted at the same time as the words leave his mouth.

'Yes, actually, I do have a question.'

Perhaps Loris is in mid-thought, or perhaps he makes a sign for Thibault to go on. Whatever he does, he still says nothing.

'What are they for, all these tubes?'

It's not a bad question and I find myself paying close attention. Eventually Loris does speak. He keeps the technical terms to a minimum and just gives the essential function of each infusion, air tube, pulse monitor and wire until I lose track. Thibault asks him for a few extra details. His interest amazes me.

The improvised lesson comes to an end and I hope that the helpful doctor will leave my room quickly. I'm scared (though of course I can't actually feel it in my stomach) that Thibault won't dare to say goodbye to me properly with him here. But, once again, his behaviour surpasses everything I would have expected of him.

'Goodbye, Elsa,' he whispers, putting his lips on my cheek.

This time, I don't need to remember to try and force my brain to capture the contact. My entire being is concentrated on it. Unfortunately, I still don't feel a thing, so I make up the sensation for myself in each of its parts. Warm, gentle lips, delicate kiss.

'Were you her partner?' asks Loris.

'Why do you say "were"?' replies Thibault.

'Sorry, it's just that . . . well, it's already been a while. Maybe you've moved on. I mean, I'm sorry. It's none of my business,' he stammers awkwardly. Happily, Thibault hasn't understood what he meant. I know exactly why he said 'were'. His boss more or less sentenced me to death this morning.

I notice that Thibault doesn't answer the young doctor, neither his excuse nor his initial question. He just nods (I assume) and leaves the room. And, with this bizarre exchange, my favourite visitor is gone again.

Some time passes before I allow myself to pay full attention to the intruder. Apparently Loris still hasn't moved. I'm even wondering if I missed him leave, until I hear him move towards the window on my right. I don't know what he is up to. After a few moments I hear some movement and eventually I make out that he is on the phone.

'Yes, it's me . . . No . . . Lousy day, yep . . . The boss . . . Do I, depressed? Yes, a bit . . .'

He could have answered 'utterly' from the sound of his miserable voice. But I might be hearing wrong. Perhaps so as not to worry whoever he's speaking to, he adds: 'Oh, it's just a patient . . . Yes, on this ward. Prolonged coma . . . Her boyfriend has just left the room.'

There is your mistake, my dear house officer. Thibault is not my boyfriend; in fact we've never even met. But I have no way of making you understand that.

'Uh . . . Yes, I asked him but he didn't answer. He just kissed her on the cheek, but it was obvious that he wanted to kiss her properly. And he probably didn't dare because I was there . . . Oh, it's OK. There are still a few more days for that . . .'

I block the rest out instantly for two reasons. The first is because Thibault gave the impression of wanting to kiss me 'properly'! The second because Loris has started sobbing. What's happened to him?

'Sorry, that was a terrible thing to say. But they want to unplug her! Can you imagine? I know, it's a part of my job but . . . This is tearing me apart. Oh, wait. My beeper's going.'

I had noticed the vibration sound for a little while but couldn't identify what it was.

'I'd better go . . . Yes . . . See you later . . . I love you too.' I hear a deep sigh come from my junior doctor before he closes the door behind him. I would sigh as well, if I could.

10

Thibault

I blink. The violent neon light is an excuse to avoid my mother's gaze. I'm back in the hospital, as though I had never left, and, for the second time in less than a week, I'm almost happy.

Wednesday, visiting day, has been identical to Monday so far. Work, idiotic smile noticed by colleagues, the detour to go and pick up Mum, the pause in front of room 55, her attempts to get me to go inside.

I pretend not to notice. I still have the bitter aftertaste of my semi-attempt to go in on Monday. I don't want to try again now.

And I have something much better to do.

I head to room 52. The picture is still stuck to the door under the number. Now that I've heard about the accident from her friends, I doubt that Elsa is particularly fond of that glacier. I still have some difficulty understanding her passion, especially given what it has done to her.

I start to open the door and then freeze. There's a voice inside, which has just stopped on hearing me turn the handle. It's a girl's voice. And it's not Rebecca from the first visit. I hear a chair being pushed back, and then the sound of hesitant steps. I let go of the handle, looking for somewhere to run. I am pathetic, I think to myself.

But whoever this person is, I have no desire to explain my reasons for being here to them. Or to tell another lie, or some non-committal form of the truth, or to avoid speaking at all. I've had enough. I just wanted to come and relax for a while, in a calm place. Nobody would accept that as an explanation, though. Well, no one except Rebecca and her boyfriend. Steve didn't really seem to like it much.

The staircase is too far. The girl would certainly see me running as soon as she opened the door. This is ridiculous. I throw myself onto a chair a few metres away and it seems to work. I try to look bored, hardly catching her eye. She looks like a student, about twenty; she peers down the corridor, one way and then the other, before going back in.

My shoulders sink and I sit back in the chair. I said that I find myself pathetic or ridiculous, but really I should say wretched. I come to hospital to see my brother and support my mother but all I want to do is hang out in a lifeless stranger's room, sneaking around so that nobody knows – and this is all, supposedly, in the name of tranquillity.

I'm just making one terrible mistake after another. With my brother, with my mother, with the preservation of my tranquillity. I shouldn't be subjecting Elsa to all this, just because I refuse to visit a member of my own family. She doesn't need me, and here's the proof: she had her three friends in there the other day, and now she's got another visitor.

I surprise myself by hoping the other person leaves quickly. And then I add 'selfish', after 'wretched', to the list of reproaches, and sink a little deeper in my chair.

This is the first time that I've lingered in the corridor on the fifth floor, so I look around the place. First, my eyes rest on the door to the staircase. I could still seek refuge there, but, even sitting here on the hard plastic, I don't have the heart to get up again. There's a window at one end, two swing doors at the other, which must lead on to the next antiseptic corridor, and a few dull-looking tables. The faded pink of the paint on the walls is vomit-inducing. I can't understand why they insist on so many pastel colours. Maybe they're afraid of shocking the patients with anything too vibrant. Although perhaps it could work the other way round if they livened the place up . . . Oh, I don't know. I've never been in a coma, or in post-coma rehabilitation. I have no idea what effect colours have on people. In any case, I'm going off on a tangent here. If what I'm doing is sitting here, imagining how I'd feel about paint colours if I were plunged into a coma, I really do have a problem.

I realise that my eyes have been resting on something for a little while. I'm looking at another number, 55. I almost leap out of my skin when I realise that my chair is placed very close to it. I've been ten centimetres away from my brother's door for the last few minutes. I think it's quite an achievement to have stayed here all this time, even without knowing it. Here is my actual problem: room 55 and its occupant.

If it weren't for him, why on earth would I be wondering what it's like to be in a coma? Excuses, police, explanations, signed confessions, and two young lives wasted. That's all I've thought about since he woke up. But what would it actually be like to be in my brother's place? To have drunk too much one night, knowing it was dangerous. To have run over two girls without even really noticing I'd done it. Apparently he almost fainted when they told him what had happened after he woke up. Good. I hope he got the fright of his life.

And the time when he was inactive in the bed, lost somewhere in his thoughts while his body recovered, what must that have done to him? How did that feel? Did he feel anything? Did he relive anything? What do you do when you're in a coma? Do you think? Do you hear other people? The doctors told me to speak to him, but I couldn't say a word.

With Elsa it took me less than two minutes to start talking.

But Elsa's done nothing wrong. Whereas my brother . . .

A noise disturbs my thoughts. I roll my head slowly to one side while still leaning against the wall. My heart beats faster as I realise that it's my mother's voice I can hear through the crack in the door. She is persistent. She never closes this door, as though she's still hoping that I'll change my mind and wander in.

I lift my arm blindly, trying to reach the handle to close the door once and for all, when I hear my name. I've been trying to ignore whatever they're saying inside, but I can't ignore the sound of my own name.

'. . . still doesn't want to come.'

'Am I not his brother any more?'

'You can't blame him for being confused.'

I notice that my mother hasn't really answered the question. Perhaps because she is not sure of the answer, or because she doesn't want to say it out loud. I don't even know what I would have said myself. It's true that I've hated him since he caused this accident, but we still share a surname, we still have the same mother. In a basic, fundamental way we'll always be family.

Except that I don't feel as though we are a family any more. A family has love and respect; it lives through highs and lows, but there always has to be some kind of basic harmony and understanding. Like Gaëlle and Julien. My brother has sunk a hundred metres below ground level, and I have no desire to help my mother drag him back up to the surface. He got down there all by himself, he'll have to dig himself out alone.

'. . . frightened.'

I open my eyes at once – that was my brother's voice again. In spite of myself, I listen.

There's a long silence. My mother hasn't answered, or perhaps she just murmured something. My hand is still suspended above the door handle, my breath suspended in my throat.

'I was frightened before. And I'm still frightened.'

The little air that is left in my lungs is stuck there and I feel as though a trickle of cold water is being poured over my entire body. I start to cough uncontrollably and cover my face with my hands. Even if I had wanted to hear the next part of the conversation, I wouldn't have been able to. In any case, at this moment I see the girl come out of Elsa's room.

With the breath still caught in my throat, I watch her go to the lifts. As soon as the doors close, I leap out of my chair and hurry over to room 52.

I turn the handle as though my life depended on it and close the door, leaning back against it with relief. My muscles are so tense you'd think that I had done battle with a tiger to get into the room. In here there's only the electrical whirr of the machines attached to Elsa. But the thoughts I tried to leave out in the corridor are still with me.

If my brother was frightened, he deserved it. If he's still frightened, he still deserves it. But perhaps it shows some regret.

I shake my head, clenching my fists. I refuse to make excuses for him, or to make room for some kind of redemption. I want to continue to hate him for what he has done. But it's true that he is still my brother. So perhaps it's impossible for me to hate him through and through.

That doesn't make sense to me either. Nothing makes sense, except being in room 52. And I'm here, and the smell of jasmine is gently soothing my mind and making me breathe easier. I've found my lighthouse, the luminous signal that brings me back to dry land after a voyage in deep water. This is my refuge, and it's a lot better than sitting in a stairwell.

Better, too, than a chair in the corridor beside the abyss into which my brother has fallen.

'Here, I bought you this.'

Julien hands me a book with a yellow and black cover before he even says hello. There's still snow on his hat and his cheeks are red from the cold. I arrived at the pub a few minutes before him, so I've already had time to defrost.

'What is it?' I ask, taking his jacket and putting it on the bench next to me.

'Read the title, that should answer all your questions.'

Julien strips off layer after layer until he is left in just a T-shirt. I pick the book up from the table. *Comas for Dummies*. Who would dare publish a book with this title? I put it down and concentrate on Julien. He has just ordered for us both and is settling back into his chair.

'I didn't think you'd be able to come,' I tell him, almost apologetic.

'I negotiated an hour with Gaëlle. It's the best I could do. Although, there might be a way we can make it a bit longer.'

'What's that?' I ask, hopefully, because I really don't want to go home straight away.

'Gaëlle has suggested that you come home with me again, like last Wednesday.'

Her concern is touching, but I decline the invitation. 'I can't come and squat at yours every time I have a bad day. I'll just have to get over it. I should have been miserable yesterday, or tomorrow when you aren't busy.'

'That's not how it works though, is it? You can't schedule these things. And, you know Gaëlle, there is a little deal to be negotiated into this.'

'What deal?'

'The same as last time: that you'll give Clara her night bottle. With one small extra thing . . .'

Julien adds the last bit with a cheeky smile. The penny starts to drop. Gaëlle's large/small scale has always been completely back to front.

'Go on then, what is this gigantic extra thing she wants from me?'

'Well, it's actually a gigantic extra thing we both want from you.'

'Well, there's a turn-up for the books,' I joke.

'We want you to take Clara for the weekend.'

'What?'

My 'what' sounds a bit like a duck being strangled, and several drinkers on neighbouring tables turn to see what's going on. I ignore them and carry on staring at Julien, as though he has just told me he's planning to grow another head.

'Are you mad? A whole weekend?'

'Only from Friday night to Sunday night,' he perseveres. 'You'd stay at ours – it's easier for you to come to us with an overnight bag than for Clara to come to yours with the entire contents of our apartment in tow. Gaëlle can explain how the bottles work and all the rest. But you already know most of it.'

'Julien, every time I've given Clara a bath or anything like that, you've been there. I mean, if anything went wrong how could you fix it if you were miles away? Where are you going, anyway?'

'Gaëlle's booked a gîte in the mountains.'

'So I'd have no means of contacting you . . .'

'We're not going to the end of the earth,' Julien laughs, 'and there is phone signal up there. But we know you'll be fine.'

'You're definitely the only ones that think so.' I take a large swig of my pineapple juice. Even its sweetness can't eclipse the terror I feel at the thought of being responsible for Clara for two whole days. 'Can't you ask Gaëlle's parents?'

'They're not available, and she wants to test you out.'

That doesn't surprise me, coming from Gaëlle, and I even manage a smile. It was Julien's idea to suggest me as Clara's godfather. I don't think Gaëlle was quite convinced at first. When I accepted, I never imagined the initiation process I'd have to go through. Up until now, I think I've passed all the tests, but this must be the last one, the ultimate one which will decide if I'm to be trusted or not. Even though I know that there aren't many alternatives now, with the christening less than two weeks away.

'Tell Gaëlle I'll do it.'

'Are you sure?' Julien asks, grinning.

'Yes, it's fine, but she'll have to give me a full demo tonight. If I'm being assessed I want to come prepared.'

'She's going out tonight, so I'll sneak you the answers,' he laughs.

'Ah, that's why you've only got an hour?'

'Exactly. Girls' night.'

'She gets about a bit, that wife of yours!'

'And so do I – this is the second time I've shirked my fatherly duties to come out and see you,' he reminds me.

'That's true.'

With business concluded, we move onto other things. I discreetly slid *Comas for Dummies* onto the bench at the start of our conversation so that it wouldn't be in Julien's eye-line, in case he was tempted to deviate onto that subject. I succeed in avoiding any questions about Elsa, and concentrate exclusively on the weather, my brother, the office, and my brother again, until our glasses are empty and Julien's hour is over.

We go in my car and, when we reach their apartment building, we have to run up the stairs. Julien's eyes are glued to his watch, he knows what he's in for if he goes beyond the time limit – Gaëlle has had him on a tight leash ever since her pregnancy. He is already on the third floor before I have reached the second. Another reminder that I ought to be getting more exercise.

I hear Gaëlle open the door and congratulate us on arriving in the nick of time. I've barely got my breath back on the doorstep when she puts Clara into my arms.

'Wait! I've still got my cold, snowy jacket on, she'll freeze!'

'With the Babygro she's wearing, no chance,' answers Gaëlle. 'But if you're not quick about sorting yourself out, she might start crying.'

I push Julien aside to get into the living room as fast as possible. Gaëlle gives me no respite; anyone would think my weekend had started two days in advance. I undress awkwardly, trying to hold onto Clara at the same time. I feel like a high-performance juggler.

This game must amuse Clara because I can see the corners of her mouth lift as I pass her from one side to the other while I struggle to get my arms out of my clothes. I even manage to take my shoes off with one hand, and I hear the laughter coming from the hallway. Gaëlle and Julien are watching me. Apparently the test is underway.

Gaëlle waves at me and then kisses Julien. I look away so as not to intrude on their brief farewell, which is not actually that brief. When it looks as though the kiss is going in quite another direction I move further into the other room. I don't blame Julien, I've seen the outfit Gaëlle is wearing under her coat; she looks stunning.

When Julien comes in after closing the door, he has the daft smile of a happy man on his face and his hair is slightly ruffled. I pass Clara to him so that I can finish taking off my jumper and then I take her back while he takes off his jacket. It must be a funny picture, from the outside. Two blokes passing a baby between them. We could be a double act.

I follow him into the bathroom and watch him bathing his daughter. My little lesson begins, and I take the reins for a minute while he goes to look for some clean pyjamas.

'So, how was today's visit?' he asks, rummaging through a cupboard.

'I didn't see my brother.' I feel bad not quite telling him the truth. He deserves better.

'I'm not talking about your brother, Thibault.'

He's a sly dog, that Julien. He hasn't lost sight of the main topic of the evening for a moment. He's just been lulling me into a false sense of security and waiting for the time when I'm too distracted to evade his question. I take Clara out of the water and put her delicately onto the towel. She waves her little arms at me.

'Same as the other times. I slept,' I say, moving back to let him pass.

'So you never do anything but sleep when you see her?'

'I talk a bit, but she doesn't exactly make much conversation in return – what do you expect me to do?'

My reply must have been adequate because Julien doesn't say anything else. He finishes dressing Clara and puts her in my arms while he sorts out the rest of the bathroom. I dance around the room with my goddaughter while he arranges the drawers and puts her toys away.

'What are you going to do?'

That's the same question I've been asking myself for days. I stop dancing, suddenly pensive.

'I don't know what I can do, but I know what I'd like to happen.'

'What?' he asks.

'I'd like her to wake up.'

'That's down to her. You know that.'

'I'm beginning to wonder.'

He takes Clara and I follow him into the living room. In two minutes and with only one hand, he has prepared everything necessary for giving her the bottle. I pick up the feeding cushion and sit beside him on the sofa.

'Here, do some revision,' he says, passing her to me, 'and that way I've got you cornered and you'll have to keep answering.'

'Answering what?'

'Well actually I haven't really got any more questions, maybe just some advice.'

'What's that?'

'Be careful.'

For a few seconds, the sound of Clara sucking on her bottle is the only sound in the room.

'Be careful about what?' I murmur, even though I know exactly what he means.

'You're falling in love with a girl you know almost nothing about. If that was the only thing you had to worry about, it would probably just about be OK, but you're also falling in love with a girl who might never wake up.'

'What do you know about it?'

'I know what you've told me, Thibault. There's apparently no improvement, and I think you're very caught up in this for someone who only came across this girl a week ago.'

'I know.'

I do know. It's the only answer I can give. Eventually I manage to say, 'I get you,' but Julien knows that. I've understood, listened to, analysed and digested each of his words already, because they've already been going through my head for a little while.

'But I'd still like her to wake up.'

11

Elsa

The scraping of the door handle wakes me. I know at once that it's the cleaning lady. Her footsteps, her trolley, her radio. It's night-time, between midnight and one in the morning. It didn't take me long to work out why the cleaning was done at this time each night. This is the one place in the hospital where there's no risk of waking most of the patients.

She passes the broom quickly under my bed, spending a bit longer on the edges of the room. I had visitors today, my sister and Thibault, so she will almost certainly have to use the mop.

I like being woken by the cleaning lady, because of her radio, though 'woken' is rather a grand way of putting it. Apart from the commentary of the DJ, who seems to be about as asleep as everyone else at this time of night, the music she listens to isn't bad. It makes me laugh to myself inside my head to think that I am up to date with the latest hits. If I get out of here I'll know the words to all these songs. That would surprise everyone.

The cleaning lady goes into the little bathroom, only used by my visitors – I hear her grumbling that they could use the bathroom on the corridor, but she cleans it all the same. That takes about two songs and an ad break.

When the music comes back on she is on her way back into the bedroom. It's a song I love. I wish I could hum along. It reminds me of some of my best moments out on the glacier. I lose myself for a few minutes, remembering the return journeys from my climbs, when I allowed myself to sing. I only ever sang on the descent, when the hard part was over, but that always meant that it had gone well.

Yes, for the length of a song I can forget where I am and feel normal . . .

I know the tune and most of the lyrics by heart, so I sing along in my head. I can hear the mop passing back and forth on the floor. If I were the cleaning lady, I would at least mop in time with the music. She breaks up the rhythm with her random swipes, and her tired little sighs. But then she stops suddenly, and the broom handle falls sharply to the floor. I'm not too worried, I would have heard if she'd had a fall. But she seems to have frozen to the spot. Suits me, I suppose – it means I can hear the song better.

'*Santo Dios!*'

Her whisper is so charged with fear that, reluctantly, I leave my mental repetition of the chorus. What could she have seen that has alarmed her so much? I can't feel the visceral sensation of fear, but I can still imagine what it provokes in me. A tingling feeling in the stomach, a sudden chill on the nape of the neck, my breathing reduced to a single stream of air, and my whole body tense, searching for the slightest sign or detail that can rationalise this fear, and make it go away again. But I suppose that reaction is particular to me, because I hear the cleaning lady leave the room in big strides. I can hear her rubber-soled shoes squeaking very fast all the way down the corridor, before the door to my room has even swung closed.

But she has left the radio, so I can carry on listening to it in peace. The song finishes and the next is one that I like less.

The door opens again, and, pointlessly, I command my brain to use all its power to identify the people coming in. Turn your head, lift your chest, open your eyes, and then send back all the information you capture. Of course, I don't do any of that, but I imagine myself doing it. Since Monday, I have integrated this process into my every waking moment; it has become almost automatic in the space of two days.

I listen attentively to what's happening around me. There are two people: the cleaning lady and someone else. They whisper at first, so it's hard to make out properly what they're saying, but as soon as the door is closed and they come further into the room, the volume of their voices rises.

'I'm telling you that I heard something!' insists the cleaning lady.

'Maria, I'm afraid that's impossible.'

At least this conversation has enabled me to discover the name of the person I listen to the radio with, but it's the sizzling crackle of what she is saying that compels me to keep listening.

'Well I'm telling you that I didn't dream it, Doctor! I heard a noise and it came from her.'

'Maria, excuse me if I allow myself to doubt you.'

This time, I hear the voice more clearly and it's definitely my house officer and defender. I was right to think that his boss was going to put him on night shifts. I suppose he hasn't had cause to come in before because nothing ever happens.

'You don't believe me?' Maria asks with incredulity.

Her Spanish accent perfectly suits the mental picture I had made of her. And now I imagine her, eyes narrowed, scrutinising the junior doctor as though she were about to reduce him to a pot of ashes for daring to doubt her. But Loris won't allow himself to be intimidated.

'Maria, this woman's case is hopeless. There's nothing more we can do for her.'

'What? Are you telling me that you're going to give up on her, like Madame Solange next door?'

'Jesus, Maria! Do you know the names of all the people in here?'

'Do not take the Lord's name in vain, Loris. And yes, I know your name as well,' she adds, like a knight drawing her sword before an adversary. 'What did you think? That we all refer to people as numbers like you do? Not everyone has patients who can't answer back!'

'Are you saying that you would prefer to work somewhere else?'

Maria's intake of breath is as deep as mine would have been. But the doctor finally answers her question.

'Yes, we are going to disconnect her.'

'When?'

'We don't know yet.'

'Why?' persists Maria, now like an NYPD cop, dogged, mid-interrogation.

'Because it is impossible for her to come back to us.'

'What do you know about it?'

'Medicine is a science, Maria! And I'm not about to give you a course in it now. You can read the clipboard at the end of the bed if you like. There was a comment added there at the beginning of the week. Go ahead, have a look!'

Loris's exasperation is now evident. I hear Maria petulantly detaching the clipboard from its hook. She doesn't hide her fury either.

'Look on the first page, the comment at the bottom, in the right-hand margin.'

'I can't see anything,' Maria retorts.

'Yes, you can see it. You just don't know what it means.'

'These scribblings here? Could say anything.'

'It says "minus X". We put an "X" to indicate that we are waiting to know exactly how many days remain, the time during which the family decides.'

'I don't believe you. No one could be that heartless.'

'It's the truth. It was me who had to write it there. I don't like it any more than you do, but that's how it goes.'

'That's how it goes?' repeats my heroic cleaning lady. 'You know what, Loris?'

'What?'

'You disappoint me.'

I prepare myself for what's coming next, sure that the young doctor will defend himself by saying that the opinion of a cleaning lady is of little importance to him, but I'm surprised when silence follows instead. Relative silence, because the radio is still playing.

'I disappoint myself as well, Maria, but what can I do?'

I wonder if he's going to start crying again. I hope for his sake that he manages to keep it together.

'You could behave like a man, Loris, rather than a puppet. Now, just listen to me and do what you like with what I'm about to say. I was mopping and I heard a noise. It wasn't the mop. It wasn't the radio. It wasn't just her breathing. It sounded as though there was a word behind it, as though she was trying to say something.'

'Her vocal cords won't be able to function after such a long period of inactivity.'

'I didn't say that she spoke,' says Maria, 'I said that she was trying to.'

There is an irritated sigh from Loris. I hear him shuffle his feet, and then he stops.

'Very good, Maria. You've persuaded me to give her a quick check over. But I'm really only doing it so you'll leave me in peace.'

'Ah, there's a good man!'

I can hear a little smile of victory in her reply and I can hear the resignation in his. He gets two or three things out of his pocket while Maria goes back to her trolley as though nothing has happened. During this time, I hang on to the little glimmer of hope that this conversation has given me. If she isn't making it up, it means that I managed to make my lips move, all thanks to that song.

I hear the doctor bend over me. I think he must be touching me; he has pulled back the covers. But I am only half paying attention; my entire concentration is focused on the song that has just been playing. I go through the words and the tune in my head. In my mind I scream almost the whole song, but it's fair to assume that nothing leaves the confines of my head because Loris completes his examination with another sigh.

'I am sorry, Maria, but nothing has changed. Believe me, I would have loved it to be different. No, please don't say anything else.'

She must have been about to protest.

'I'm going back to my room now. Don't hesitate to call me if something real happens.'

'It was real.'

'According to you, yes. But I'm telling you that it is impossible.'

'According to you,' she repeats.

Loris leaves. Then so does Maria with her trolley.

I'll come back to my little glimmer of hope in the morning. For the moment, I wish I could cry.

12

Thibault

All this snow. I've been crawling along behind a snow plough three cars ahead for ages and Julien told me to be there for six, which is in ten minutes. If it goes on like this I'll arrive at midnight and fail the weekend test before it's even started. And from the looks of the white blanket layering itself across the road, things aren't going to speed up any time soon.

I resign myself to defeat when my mobile phone rings. It's Julien. I grit my teeth and answer, gabbling excuses before he has a chance to say a word.

'Jules, I'm so sorry, I'm never going to get there for six. I left work on time, and I had everything ready in the car so that I wouldn't have to go back to mine first, but . . .'

He is laughing on the other end of the line.

'Wait, where are you?' I ask.

'Stuck in my car, same as you!'

'What? You've already left? Is Clara at home alone? No. Of course not,' I correct myself immediately. 'Have you taken her with you after all?'

'Thibault, what are you talking about? We're sticking to the original plan, nothing's changed! It's just that with all this snow I had a few extra things to get before we left, so I'm stuck in traffic like you. Bloody snow plough!'

'Are you stuck behind a snow plough as well?'

'I'm two cars behind you, Einstein!'

I turn around and see Julien through the windscreen of the car between us and wave at him. He flashes his headlights back at me. The driver of the car between us looks confused, but then realises that the waving and flashing aren't meant for him.

'I'm saved then!' I say, turning back to the road.

'I'd say so, yes. In any case, Gaëlle is so excited about this weekend away, she's not going to let a little fifteen-minute delay put her off.'

'But what about the road?'

'I've called the gîte where we're staying and they say it's not snowing there yet, apparently it's forecast to start in the middle of the night.'

'Oh that's good. Still, you'd better be careful, it could be slippery getting up there.'

'Since when have you been so interested in the snow?'

I know what he is trying to suggest, so I think about this for a few moments before saying: 'My best mate and his wife are setting out in weather like this, while I'm left holding the baby. What would happen to her if anything happened to you two?'

'So nice of you to be concerned,' he says, before turning serious. 'You do know that being her godparent could involve that sort of thing though, don't you, if anything were ever to happen to us? When you come to the ceremony in the church next week, you're committing to always being there for our little angel, you know!'

'Yes, I'm trying not to think about that,' I joke, half-heartedly. 'Anyway, it's not actually written anywhere that it's me who's responsible for Clara in that type of situation, is it?'

'Did Gaëlle not talk to you about this?'

Julien's tone makes me uncomfortable.

'What, what are you saying?'

'Nothing, don't worry, I'm just kidding!'

'Right.' My heart is beating really fast. I realise that I am actually frightened. Work responsibilities: no problem. Professional engagements: fine. But personal life: since Cindy, the whole thing is still in pieces. I have no idea where to start.

'Thibault, are you still there?'

'I'm still here, yep.' I must have gone quiet for a second for Julien to ask me that. 'I just don't like using the phone while I'm driving,' I say, by way of an excuse.

'Oh, you mean the two metres an hour you're moving at the moment – do you think they're going to pull you over for that? Honestly, if you see a policeman doing anything but trying to get the traffic moving, bring him to me!'

'Even so, is there anything else we urgently need to talk about right this moment?'

'You haven't seen Cindy again recently, have you?'

This question takes me by surprise. In fact I'm probably making a face a bit like a toad who's just swallowed his tongue. 'How did you know that?' I splutter.

'Because I saw her today, and because suddenly you sound even shakier than you did before when I mention your godfathering responsibilities.'

He knows me so well.

'How did that go then?' he continues.

I think for a moment. How *did* it go?

'Bad,' I begin. 'Rotten. She was different, kind of tarty, pathetic.'

'Wait, Thibault – where did you see her, what are you talking about exactly?'

'She paid a late-night visit to my apartment. A very badly-judged surprise!' I can hear my own anger. Even a week later, I still haven't quite got my head around the encounter.

'Tell me more.'

'Well, she was clearly bored at home by herself and wanted some company. Is that enough information for you?'

'She did that? I'd never have believed it.'

'There are lots of things we wouldn't believe other people would do.'

'And what did *you* do?'

'I kicked her out, what do you think?'

For a split second I'm really cross with Julien for thinking I could succumb to Cindy's charms again but then my anger evaporates. The state I'm in at the moment, it could easily have happened.

'Sorry, Thibault,' he says.

'No problem.'

'Yes, there is a problem. I was ready to believe that

something might have happened, with the way you've been feeling recently, but I ought to know better.'

'Well you realised it, that's what counts. And, to be honest, she might have got what she wanted if I hadn't come to my senses in time.'

We go quiet again. Two friends thinking their own thoughts, in silence, on the phone to each other. I doubt that girls could ever imagine how things work inside our heads. Men are often accused of being empty vessels, or having one-track minds, but my mind is in a constant state of chaos, going down several tracks all the time. It must be the same for Julien. We each sit there, not saying anything, but hanging onto our phones like a pair of lemons. People might be partly right about us, I think – not about being shallow, they're wrong there – my problem is that although I can identify this chaos inside my head, I have absolutely no idea what to do about it.

We're saved by the snow plough thirty seconds later.

'Julien?' I say, as though nothing has happened. The snow plough parks on the pavement. 'It looks as though things are moving up ahead.'

'OK. See you in a minute! Don't worry about leaving me a space to park, just go up and tell Gaëlle I'll wait for her downstairs.'

At only ten past six, I finally get out of my car. Julien stops beside me with his hazard lights on. I wave and run into his building. The heating in my car has started working again, but you couldn't exactly call it roasting. I take the stairs two at a time to warm myself up, and make another mental note, huffing and puffing, to start jogging in the mornings.

Gaëlle opens the door in a very different outfit from the one she was wearing on Wednesday. I quickly explain the situation and she motions towards two enormous bags in the hallway. I put one on my back and pick up the other one, heading for the lift. Downstairs, Julien gets out of the car. The boot is already open. I give him the bags and remember what I had forgotten to ask him.

'Where do you keep your pushchair?'

'You mean Clara's?'

'Yes, Jules, Clara's – who else's pushchair do you think I'd be talking about?'

'Sorry,' he laughs, 'I still can't believe we're having conversations about pushchairs these days. It's folded up behind the dresser in her room. Are you thinking of taking her out in it? I don't think I've ever seen you take her out in anything but the baby carrier . . .'

'That's because I've never done it on my own before; you're always there and you always insist on strapping her into that thing.'

'Don't you find it easier?'

'Yes, I do, but I've had an idea that might involve the buggy.'

'Hmm mysterious! Anyway, you know where it is, I trust you. Don't fight too much with it to get it unfolded, if you're gentle it should just pop out by itself.'

'I think you said the same thing about the straps on the baby carrier, and it took me ages to figure out how to get them in the right place.'

'At least I haven't tried to get you to knot yourself into Gaëlle's pink scarf carrier; that would have had you running straight for the thing with the straps.'

I smile, imagining him tangled with a pink scarf around his torso. Even Julien, the baby expert, has experienced some of the less dignified challenges of parenthood.

'Right, I think Gaëlle's bag was small and, you know your wife, she'll probably want to carry it down herself. Have a great weekend, and enjoy the escape from town on my behalf as well.'

'You ought to get out for a change too, it would probably do you good,' says Julien, closing the boot.

'Yeah, but who with?' I sigh.

Julien just smiles at me before he gets into the car. I give him a last wave as I go back into the building.

'Is there anything you want me to explain again?' asks Gaëlle, when I get back up.

'No, it's fine. Get out of that door! Prince Charming is waiting down there with his trusty steed,' I say, kissing her on the cheek.

Gaëlle grabs me and gives me a big hug in return; she's always been affectionate like that.

'Thank you, Thibault,' she says into my ear. 'You don't know how happy it makes me that you're doing this for us.'

'Don't worry. It's a pleasure.'

'I hope you have a family of your own one day.'

My response is already on the tip of my tongue. The 'who with' that I used a few moments ago downstairs. But what comes out of my mouth is something completely different.

'Yes, I hope so too.'

Gaëlle doubles back and looks at me with stupefaction and amusement. I know how she feels. That's the first time I've ever admitted to it. Everyone can tell when they see me with Clara, but I've never said I wanted a baby out loud.

'I'm touched that you let me in on that secret,' she says, with a smile.

I go with her to the door and wish her a good weekend.

With all the comings and goings I haven't even had time to say hello to Clara yet. She is ensconced in her bed-playpen contraption, bobbing gently up and down. I bend over and lift her up in my arms. Wonderful little person, not a care in the world. I could learn so much from her.

I go over to the window, letting her play with my fingers. There's no way to tell whether Julien and Gaëlle have already set off, because their windows look out onto the other side of the building.

The snow continues to fall and the orange of the street-lights gives the town a strange glowing charm. It's not even six thirty yet but, from here, you could believe that everyone was already asleep. I surprise myself with my own thoughts and Julien's question comes back into my head. Since when has the snow had this effect on me?

I do have an answer, but the thought of it frightens me, so I leave it for another time and go back to the sofa.

13

Elsa

My mother and father are in my room and they're not alone. The consultant is here with them, that poisonous man who's trying to finish me off. I feel so angry just knowing he's near me, I could almost jump up just to wipe the self-satisfaction off his smug face.

Ever since he came in, it's been very obvious that he is here to talk about 'minus X', and to set the date once and for all. I know that he's already raised the idea with my parents, but I assume it was in a less drastic way than this. And even 'drastic' seems like a gentle way of putting it. If there were a single term that encompassed 'crass', 'flippant' and 'totally insensitive' all in one, I think it would perfectly describe his approach.

'You understand, madam, that there really is no further hope.'

And that stupid, obsequious language! You might as well call her 'ma'am' and be done with it. If you're going to decree my imminent demise, you could at least have the courtesy to do it with a little authenticity. Anyone would think you were a character in one of those old westerns, except that you're wearing a white coat!

Well, that's how I imagine him, anyway, this high and mighty doctor who gives me the creeps, with his coat unbuttoned, one hand resting casually on his hip, the other elbow leaning against the wall. I bet he wears jeans instead of proper trousers. Probably a scruffy old T-shirt too. Anyway, this is all my invention, but he could easily look like that. There's such an infuriating nonchalance in his voice, as though he knows it all, as though he's better than everyone else. I can't understand why my father hasn't reacted to him yet.

My mother reacted just a moment ago. She is weeping now, almost in silence. I can make out her sobs more easily when she speaks because the ends of her words get cut off.

It's strange, though. After all, she was the one who was talking about disconnecting me the other day. Given her tearful reaction now, it almost seems as though my parents' roles have reversed.

'Re-really no h-hope?' Her voice completely breaks off at the end of her question. I hope my father has had the sense to put his arms around her, or even just to hold her hand. She's in utter distress, and that doesn't happen very often. She must be panicking as well. I offer up a silent prayer that my father is behaving in a caring, husbandly way with her. I seriously doubt that my prayer has the slightest effect, but I need to know that he has at least done something.

'Anna, calm yourself, so that we can try and understand all this.'

That's reasonable advice I suppose, Dad in all his sympathetic glory, but it's not exactly what I had hoped he would say to her.

'Would you mind waiting a minute, Doctor, while my wife pulls herself together?'

The grunt from the doctor must mean yes. As I was saying . . . a real cowboy. But where has my house officer gone? He would certainly have handled this with more tact! Although, knowing him, if he saw my mother sobbing like this, they might have been wiping away a lot more tears than hers this afternoon.

The doctor leaves the room. My second prayer is to trigger some event that will result in his breaking a leg while he's outside. But, even though I try this prayer five times, nothing happens and when he comes back I don't hear the sound of crutches clicking against the floor.

'Have you had time to think?'

Oh, sure! Five minutes will certainly have been plenty of time to think this little matter over. Idiot.

I know that, rather than being annoyed, I should be putting all my energy into ordering my brain to activate and showing them that I'm back in the game, but I can't help it, all my concentration goes into emotion. It's only with Thibault that I feel any possibility of transforming these emotions into actions. Right now I'm just a useless hurricane of anger.

I wonder for a second, though . . . isn't anger a physiological chemical reaction? Which would mean that I'm making progress? But I studied geology, not medicine, so I can't really speculate. Instead I wait for my parents to reply.

'No.'

My father's voice is firm and the message is clear, even if I would have preferred him to punch the consultant's lights out. Perhaps it is my survival instinct to feel so much aggression towards this doctor. After all, my future, my life, is in the hands of this man, and whatever case he makes for me. If he manages to persuade everyone I've gone, they'll unplug me and . . .

But I can't think about what comes after that. For now, I'm still here. I can hear. And today I'm alive and I want to stay that way.

'OK,' says the doctor, 'I understand your hesitation, but do bear in mind that the longer you wait to make your decision, the more intensely you will suffer when the time comes.'

It sounds like an automated response, like one of those programmed telephone messages. 'You have reached the answerphone of Doctor so-and-so, please unplug your daughter after the beep.'

'Do you have children, Doctor?'

My father's question intrigues me. I have a feeling my fist-in-the-face may be about to materialise in the form of a cutting remark, which could have more or less the same effect.

'Yes, two.'

Liar.

There is something remarkable about having hearing as your only means of perception. It means that everything associated with sound takes on its own particular flavour. Over the past seven weeks, I've noticed myself naturally associating what people say with colours and textures. My sister's voice, brimming with lust and hormones as she recounts stories of her love life, is sickly red velvet. My mother is a sort of purple leather, trying to seem shiny and robust, but cracking and weakened all over, like a well-used handbag. This consultant is as cold and unrefined as a steel construction girder.

In the midst of all this, thankfully, a rainbow has broken out across the sky over the past ten days. Thibault has arrived with all his emotion and newness. I haven't managed to pick out any single colour from him yet. He's just shimmering and fascinating. So I've stopped at rainbow; it seems fitting. Whatever he is, he sounds better than all the rest, who mix together with their bad news to make something that looks unpalatable and ugly.

To return to the matter at hand though, this doctor is a liar. At the very least, I know that what he has just said is a lie. He does not have two children. I doubt he even has one. As far as I can tell from having listened to him, this guy might just about have a wife, but that's all. His last response was just as superficial as all the other things he's said, and just as contrived to mislead his audience.

Or, perhaps he knew what was coming next and wanted to avoid the inevitable response: 'Oh, you don't have children? Then you can't possibly imagine what it's like to have to make this decision!'

I surprise myself. This is the first reasonable thought I've had about my beloved consultant. In any case, I can't get my head around the idea that a person would become a doctor, presumably with the intention of saving lives, and then be totally indifferent, verging on enthusiastic, at the thought of terminating someone's life. How do you find a middle ground between the emotional attachment of my house officer, and the total detachment of this consultant?

Maybe it's through years of experience. It must be. I can't see how else it could happen. He must have had to make this sort of decision lots of times before. But, in spite of that, I don't get the impression that he's really given it any consideration, or tried to find another way. I know that can't be the case, but that is how it seems. At least to me, with nothing to do but listen.

My father, who has no idea that the doctor is lying to him, doesn't persevere with the verbal slap that he seemed about to deliver, and instead he continues to comfort my mother in stern whispers.

'Sir,' begins the doctor, who seems to have grasped that he won't be getting anything else out of my mother for the moment, 'here are the papers. I know that you haven't made your decision yet, but sometimes having the text in front of you helps. I'm not asking you to fill them out this evening. Just to read them. Or even just to leave them on a table so that you can go on thinking. In any case, please do not hesitate to call me, whatever the time. My contact details are at the bottom. Contact me any time, I mean it. If I'm busy, I may not be able to answer. But this number is reserved for this type of situation, and I do all I can to be on hand for the families of patients.'

This time, I'm not sure what to think. I think I am learning something about neutrality. The way the doctor is speaking sounds professional. Even though I would prefer that it were the junior doctor who was taking care of all this. At least I've heard him say 'I love you' to someone. That shows he has a beating heart. I'm not saying the consultant doesn't have a heart, but rather that he has encased it in the stark grey metal that I associate with his voice.

My father takes the papers and the consultant says goodbye to my parents. I hear vague murmurs from them, but then only my mother's sobs. My father must be stroking her hair. She calms down after a while, and comes over to my bed. Maybe she takes my hand, maybe she just looks at me. I don't hear much else. I am falling asleep.

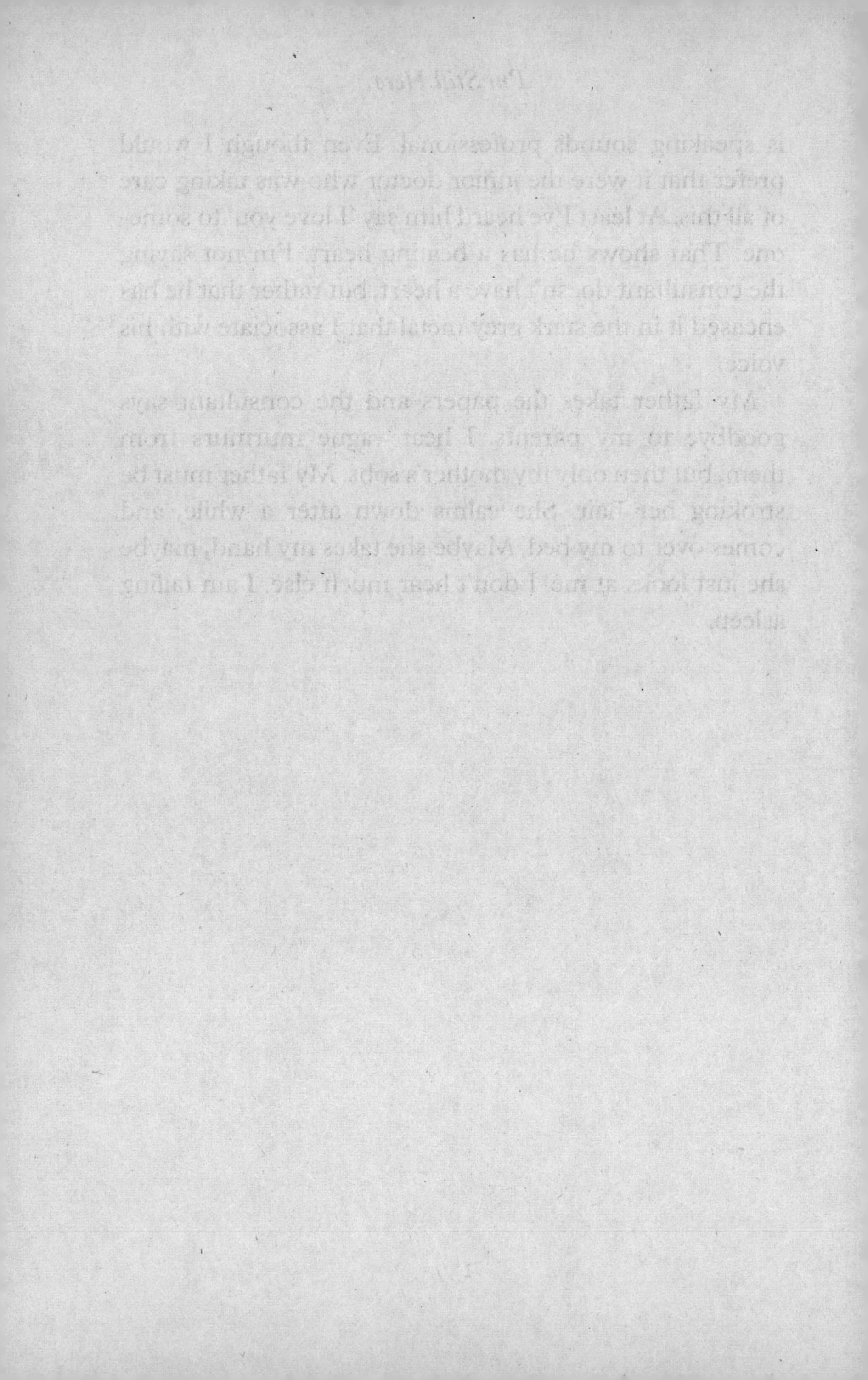

14
Thibault

'Damn you, Julien! Argh!'

The curse comes straight back to me like a boomerang when, a second after shouting this, my finger is pinched in the pushchair's hinge.

Clara moves around inquisitively in her cot. I put her back in there as soon as I realised that the simple flick of the buggy that Julien had promised was not going to be sufficient to make it open out. I take a step back from the wreckage and look at my watch. At this rate, I'll never have enough time to get it all done. Never mind, I'll have to try again later.

I open the cupboard and get out the baby carrier and its straps. At least I won't have to fight with this one. I glance back at the buggy, which remains resolutely folded. *Just you wait till tonight, my friend. Tonight I'll find the instruction manual and we'll really see who's boss.* I have no intention of disturbing Gaëlle and Julien to ask them to help me, so it'll be a solo mission, but I think the booklet I saw on a table in the other room should make an excellent battle companion.

I put on the baby carrier without any trouble and do up all the necessary buckles. I pop Clara into it, after a moment spent covering her gorgeous little face with kisses, and readjust it to fit her. We're ready to go out. I'm proud of myself, in spite of my stinging failure with the buggy.

Outside, everything is grey. The snow that fell last night has already melted around the tyres of cars and buses, and what remains has lost its lustre in the haze of exhaust fumes. The sky looks ominously dull.

It's frightening how much the weather can change in a single day. Last night it was snowing, and today it looks as though there's a storm coming. That's why I wanted to take the buggy out, because it has a plastic hood which would protect Clara if it started to rain. But instead I've got a big umbrella, which will keep us both dry if necessary. I suppose I could always stow her away under my raincoat if I needed to, but I'm sure the umbrella will be enough.

I walk along the de-snowed pavement. It's no bad thing that the snow has melted because it could have been slippery otherwise and that would have slowed me down considerably, especially with Clara strapped to my front. I catch the eyes of several women my age and their glances linger, drawn by what must be some kind of Dad-skier allure. After the hat, the jacket, the gloves, the scarf and the snow boots, there is only Clara to show that I'm not about to hit the slopes.

Every time a woman smiles, my internal gamebook takes me to page 60: 'Smile Politely Back, You Never Know'. I force myself to turn the page and read the next instruction ('Go on Your Way'), asking myself what is so extraordinary about seeing an over-dressed man carrying a baby. I could add the epithet 'extraterrestrial', after 'Dad-skier'.

The journey to the hospital is a lot shorter from Julien's house. No need to take the car, no need either to collect my mother. I arranged it with her. Or rather, she arranged it with a friend. Clara was my excuse not to have to join them on the visit to my brother today. I just had to wait until my mother would have finished and left the hospital. Now it's four in the afternoon, it should be perfect. With any luck, the friend who went with her will have invited her back to her house. Perhaps they'll have dinner together. That would do my mother good. It would do everyone good.

I get to the hospital quickly. Clara is looking around her with eyes full of curiosity. At that age, everything must seem interesting. With the layers I put on her, and our brisk walk, neither she nor I has had the chance to get cold on the way here.

I opt for the lift instead of the stairs. Once again, I notice the meaningful glances from the women standing with me in this confined space. They seem to be women of all ages, in fact. I make eye contact with one woman in her thirties. She is very pretty, radiant even, and she seems pleased, full of hope somehow, to see me with Clara. I don't understand her interest until I see her get out of the lift at the maternity ward.

When we arrive at the fifth floor I hardly have to lift my little finger before everyone gets out of the way, pressing themselves against the walls to let me out. It is such a foreign experience that I burst out laughing as soon as the metal doors slide closed behind me.

'Do you see the effect we're having on them?' I say to Clara, tapping her on the nose.

Suddenly I hear a familiar voice. I raise my eyes and all my light-heartedness immediately drains away. At the end of the corridor my mother is pushing a wheelchair. In the chair is a man, my brother. It was his voice I recognised. I look quickly around me. The staircase is several metres away, but I hardly have the chance to take a step in that direction when my mother spots me from down the hall.

'Thibault?'

I hear the surprise in her voice, and a whole range of other things as well. It is a mother's gift, or maybe a woman's, to be able to fit an entire dictionary's worth of meaning into a single word. I know that in her 'Thibault?' there is: What are you doing here? Why have you come? Have you changed your mind about your brother? It's Clara! She's gorgeous, let me come and say hello! How did you get here? You told me you weren't coming! And that's just for starters.

I stand still, planted like a tree, to wait for the little cortège to come and join me.

'Here,' she says as she gets closer, 'this is Amelie, the friend who brought me. We stayed at hers for a little while, that's why I'm here so late. Were you looking for me?'

Without knowing it, my mother has just given me my excuse. I had absolutely no idea how I was going to explain my presence at the hospital.

'I tried to find you at home and you weren't there. I was worried. Normally you're home by now.'

'Oh, silly boy,' she says, putting her hand to my cheek. 'I could have been with Amelie, you know that. Why didn't you try my mobile?'

'You always leave it switched off, Mum, it didn't even occur to me.'

'What was the point of me buying you that phone?'

The voice that has just inserted itself into the conversation feels like a punch in the stomach. I close my eyes and take a deep breath. Until now, Clara has blocked my vision of the silhouette in the chair my mother is pushing. But now that my brother has spoken, I can't go on ignoring him. I open my eyes and slowly lower my gaze towards him.

'Hello, Sylvain.'

'Hi, Thibault! Haven't seen you around here for a while!'

I want to sigh heavily but I hold myself back. My brother sounds the same as ever. I don't know why I even bothered to hope that the accident might have changed him. You can never have a sincere conversation with him; he is absolutely incapable of saying anything without being irreverent.

'I wonder why,' I retort, holding his gaze.

Sylvain doesn't look much like me. His blond hair has always been more obedient than mine, for a start, and his blue eyes have brought many more girls to their knees than mine could ever dream of doing. I see the scars across his cheeks. Another on the bridge of his nose. I let my gaze wander over the rest of his body. An arm in plaster, and both of his legs. The doctor said that the car's dashboard had literally snapped across his knees. I had a knee injury once and the pain was almost unbearable. No wonder my brother lost consciousness and went into a coma for six hours. He must really have suffered. But that doesn't excuse him.

'As friendly as ever,' he replies.

I was prepared for an insolent reply, but his tone is more detached than I expected. You'd almost think he was hurt. It's not like him at all. He must be trying to get rid of me.

'And you're as *carefree* as ever,' I answer, dryly.

'That's enough, you two.'

I would have expected those words to come from my mother, but no. It's her friend who speaks up, her eyes moving from my brother to me with obvious reproach. I understand why a second later when I see my mother's white knuckles gripping the handles of the wheelchair.

'Sorry, Mum, didn't mean to . . .'

My brother and I speak at exactly the same time and, for the first time in this encounter, I feel the family link that unites us. The words came out of our mouths in unison and my mother's eyes widen, but the magic doesn't last. In the next breath, it's all gone.

I put my hand on hers to reassure her. She looks at me with tears in her eyes. I kiss her on the cheek and whisper in her ear.

'Sorry, Mum, I'm still not ready for this.'

At this moment Clara starts to wriggle. My mother's attention is immediately turned towards her, and so is Amelie's, and I find myself answering all their questions about her health, her parents, their weekend, and how I am coping with her. They share stories about how they managed with their own children as babies, and I listen with half an ear, my eyes fixed on the tiny hand playing with the zip on my jacket.

'Are Julien and Gaëlle well?' asks my brother, his voice lowered now.

This new way of speaking is radically different from the one I have always associated with him. I can't decide whether it annoys me or not.

'What are you trying to do then, little monkey?' I say, still looking at Clara.

'Stop it, Thibault. At least answer my question.'

'They're fine.'

'And you're their babysitter now, when they go away?'

'As you can see.'

'Thibault . . .' he sighs.

That must be the first time I've ever heard him sigh. Normally, he sniggers constantly, and there's a smug smile that I've always wished I could wipe off his face. This at least sounds more sincere. Perhaps I should make an effort.

'For today, yes, it's the first time.'

'You look as though you know what you're doing.'

His voice surprises me again and makes me lower my eyes towards him. He is looking strangely at Clara. It's not the same as the way I look at her, but nevertheless I think I see some affection and maybe regret in his expression. Fleetingly.

'Are you in training?' he says, laughing again.

His laughter is clearly not genuine. It's as though he is hiding behind it, like a bad joke. A very bad joke, in fact, because a moment later his face takes on a look of utter devastation. I'm having a lot of trouble interpreting his behaviour. I don't know how to respond.

I could answer no, but I don't want to say anything that could spark a tirade of mockery. I could answer yes but it might provoke any number of other questions. I choose my words carefully.

'I'm enjoying myself.'

I think I have just surprised my brother for the first time in a long while. He doesn't respond, but just stares at Clara and me. And then his eyes break away and are lost somewhere at the end of the corridor. My stomach tenses strangely, and my throat tightens. I realise that I want to go on talking to him, but I don't know what to say. So I don't say anything and instead wait for my mother and her friend to finish their little discussion.

'Are you coming downstairs with us?' she asks.

'I. . .'

'You're not staying up here, are you?'

'I just want to . . . digest all this.'

I glance at my brother. He is still staring at the end of the corridor. There's only a window down there, but I doubt he's actually paying attention anyway; he seems to be watching the clouds pass. He is lost in thought. My mother did say that he was using the time to think. Maybe she is right to believe in him. In any case, I've never actually succeeded in having a real conversation with him before.

'Well . . . whatever you think is best,' begins my mother. 'Will you at least come down in the lift with us?'

Luckily, I've already managed to think of a way to stay in the hospital without anyone knowing. 'I always take the stairs, you know that.'

'Ah.'

I faintly perceive her disappointment, but even if I had intended to leave, I would have said the same. She smiles sadly at me and leans on the wheelchair to make it move. Her friend nods her head at me. My brother's eyes are still staring into the distance.

I stay still until they've deposited my brother and the doors of the lift are closing behind them, my mind in turmoil. As soon as I hear the doors click, it's as though I'm a clock which has just been reset. I stroke Clara's bonneted head distractedly and start to walk towards my destination. I've already spotted the photo of mountains that is Sellotaped between the two numbers. I know that photo by heart now. I even think I know where it was taken – I spent several hours looking for it online last weekend.

I put one hand on the handle and the other on the door to push it open, and I take a deep breath. I don't know why, but I feel anxious.

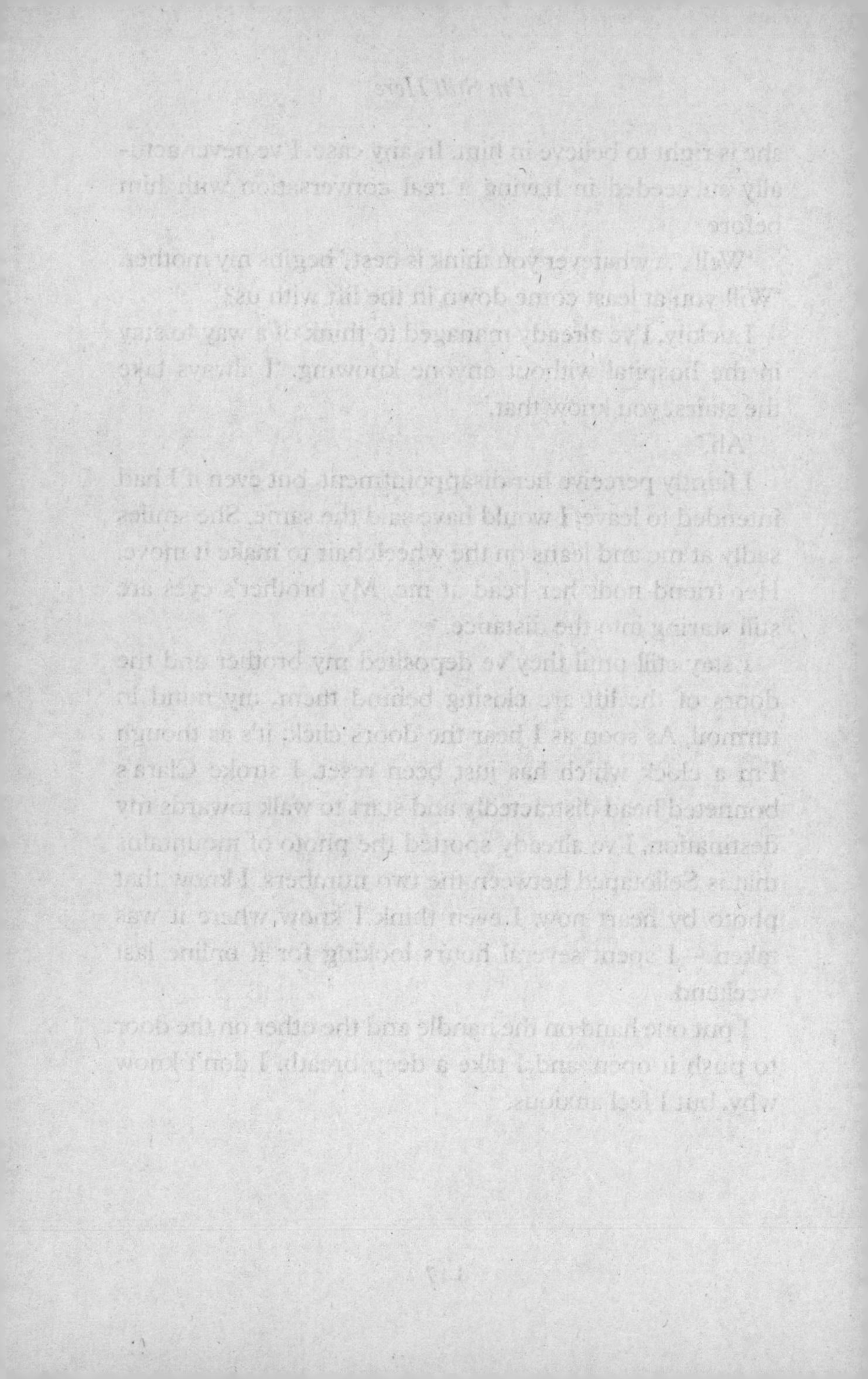

15

Elsa

A new voice. Pure and luminous, like snow that has just fallen. It's as though a golden snowflake is drifting towards me. This is almost the most wonderful sound I have ever heard, second only to the deeper voice which murmurs alongside this new one. A rainbow and a snowflake together: I don't know how they could ever coexist from a weather point of view, but they are coexisting now in my room.

A vivid image comes back to me. I have seen a rainbow and snow at the same time. Once on a glacier. It had snowed in the night, and the snow melted as the sun came up into a transparent sky. There was water flowing through the glacial rills, the currents of melted ice, snaking, sinuous all the way through the glacier. A little crack in the ice had made a mini-waterfall, just enough to make a rainbow when you looked at it from the right angle. Snow and a rainbow together. It is possible, then.

I want to smile. At my memory. At the wonderful present that Thibault has given me by bringing this brand new person with him to visit me.

Suddenly, it all collapses. Thibault has brought a baby with him. My brain immediately sets about coming up with every possible scenario that could have given rise to this situation. My morale plummets twenty metres under the ice. I feel as though I am suffocating.

I start to panic. It feels as though I am back under the avalanche in July. The atmosphere presses down on me from all sides and, like this summer, I have no way of crying out in terror. In my mind all I can perceive is chaos and destruction. It's ten days since I last had a nightmare and now, awake, I am living through the compound horror of all those days at once. Terror in its purest form.

In the midst of all this I can hear a sound, very far away, smothered by the howling wind which is buffeting me on all sides. I try to concentrate on the sound, to assign it a colour, a texture, a flavour, anything that will help me escape this anguish. I try to focus all my attention on it, blocking out the memories of my accident. But as soon as I succeed in getting them to move out of the way, they bowl back in even stronger. In my head I am screaming for someone to save me and, suddenly, everything stops.

'Elsa! Elsa! My God, what's going on?'

My rainbow stutters, his colours waver. Thibault is stricken. The baby has started to cry. This new chaos of sounds ought to be unbearable, especially so close to my ear, but no, it reassures me more than anything I can imagine. I hear a beep which comes and goes, the sound of my hair dragging across the pillow, a continuous murmur.

'Elsa! Elsa. Elsa.'

The sound of the baby's cry grows sweeter, and then all the nearby sounds overlap each other.

'I'm sorry, Clara. I was worried about Elsa. Shh, shh. There we go.'

The baby hiccups gently and calms down in a few seconds. It sounds as though I'm not the only one who is soothed by Thibault's voice.

The door of my room opens with a clatter. Hurried footsteps, it must be two people. Everything is happening very fast.

'Oh . . . *you're* here.'

My house officer. He sounds both taken aback and a little angry at once.

'Look after her!' cries Thibault. 'Who cares if I'm here or not!'

'That baby is going to put me off,' replies the junior doctor, tartly.

'Don't even think about it, I'm staying right here!'

'Doctor?'

A woman's voice. Must be the nurse whose hands have been moving about over me for the last couple of seconds.

'Yes?' he answers.

'There are a few broken attachments, but everything else seems stable.'

'What?'

'I said, everything is stable.'

'Does that mean she's OK?' Thibault cuts in.

'You're making this very difficult!' shouts Loris, almost losing his temper.

'She just had a spasm so monumental that I thought she was going to shatter into pieces!' Thibault shouts back, in a voice that sounds like a rainbow turned to red. 'How do you expect me to behave?'

'What have you done?' asks the junior doctor.

'Me? Nothing!'

'All these wires are detached and you're saying that you haven't done anything?'

'She practically sat up in the bed! That spasm was violent enough to detach all your bloody gadgets!'

'Those gadgets are the only thing keeping her alive!'

'So why is everything stable then?'

The baby starts to cry again. Thibault immediately turns his attention back to her. His murmurs take a little longer to reassure her this time, because he has just been shouting. To one side, I can hear the doctor come over to the nurse and they talk in technical terms. I hear some clicking of tubes, the drip being adjusted, the covers straightened. Little Clara is calm.

'I'm sorry,' says Loris.

I assume that I am OK. At the same time, I dare to hope that my survival instinct would be alarmed again if I was actually in danger of . . . but I cut off the ending of that thought.

'I'm sorry I was so cross,' replies Thibault, his voice back to its normal shades.

'You say that she had a spasm?' continues Loris.

'It only lasted a second, but I think that must have been the longest second of my entire life.'

'Can you describe what you saw?'

There is a brief silence, as though Thibault is gathering his thoughts. The nurse continues her work over me.

'It all happened at once. I was taking off Clara's hat and the beep of the machine that takes her pulse, the one you showed me the other day, started going really fast. The next second, Elsa just stiffened right up, unbelievable. It was very violent . . . I didn't see what happened to all the monitors and tubes, I just concentrated on her.'

'I understand.'

He gives a few instructions to the nurse, and then continues.

'Nothing in particular happened when you arrived?'

'No, nothing. Really. I had been in here for barely a minute. I hadn't even taken Clara out of the carrier. And, as you see, she's still in there. Will you give me a minute?'

'Go ahead.'

So Clara, the little golden snowflake, is strapped to Thibault's chest. That explains why the noises were so close.

'Is this your child?' asks Loris.

In a second my whole being is racing again. I feel the tempest starting to bring chaos back into my head.

'No, she's the daughter of some friends of mine.'

Everything is back in order. Clara is not Thibault's daughter. What intense relief.

As soon as I've had this thought I give myself a mental slap on the wrist. What was I thinking, getting into a state like that? What does it have to do with me whether Thibault is the father of a golden snowflake or not? I need to look at the evidence and try to get some perspective. I'm holding onto Thibault, but he doesn't belong to me.

'I see,' answers the doctor. 'You know that normally we don't allow babies to come onto this ward.'

'Ah, I didn't know that. Can we stay for now anyway?'

'Today, my eyes are closed. But not next time.'

I think the nurse has finished her checks because I hear her smoothing my covers and replacing the sensors. The metallic noise of the clipboard being replaced in its holder confirms this a few moments later.

'Doctor? Have you filled in the notes?'

'Write them for me, if you wouldn't mind.'

He dictates something in incomprehensible jargon, then signs the page that the nurse passes to him. Then she leaves the room.

Thibault must have finished arranging himself. I hear him relaxed, throwing Clara up and down in the air. I don't think he has gone so far as to remove his shoes this time, however. If he's come with a baby, he certainly isn't here to sleep.

'You haven't answered my question,' he says suddenly.

'I'm sorry?' says Loris, surprised.

'How is it possible that with all those things disconnected she can still breathe?'

'Her body can keep itself alive for around two hours. She can breathe herself and maintain her vital functions during that time. But after that she needs assistance again.'

'Is that normal?'

'It happens sometimes. It's a sign to us that the body still hasn't recovered and that the coma is still necessary.'

Without a doubt I would have preferred it to have been the junior doctor who spoke to my parents about unplugging me, rather than the consultant. He has a far less categorical way of speaking about things. He almost makes my coma sound like a natural and benign state.

'Do you have any idea how long she'll stay like this?' asks Thibault.

'I can't answer that question.'

'Why? Because you don't know?'

'Because you're not family.'

My trusty house officer sounds almost apologetic. I get the feeling that he would like to say more, but that he is holding back. 'I'll leave you with her,' he says, after a moment's hesitation. 'Have a good day.'

'You too.'

Loris leaves us alone. Clara, Thibault, and me. I am still shaken by what has just happened. Silence reigns. Even the baby's little noises are discreet. I ask myself what is happening. I have the impression that my rainbow is losing some of his shine.

16

Thibault

I need to calm down.

No, I am calm. I need to think this through properly. Julien was right: I'm falling in love with a girl who's in a coma. It's not healthy. But when I saw her just now, her eyes so huge and open, in the grip of that horrifying seizure, I reacted purely out of a reflex for someone I care about.

Reflex . . . I frighten myself, especially when a whisper involuntarily escapes my lips: 'Elsa . . . I know hardly anything about you, and yet . . .'

I leave my words hanging in the air. I'm not really talking to her, for once, so I don't feel any need to finish this comment out loud. But the end of the sentence looms inside my head. I realise that I must look about the same as my brother did out in the hallway. I can't believe I'm finding similarities between us, but I'm sure I have the same lost and faraway look he had when he was gazing out at the grey sky through the window at the end of the corridor.

Clara fidgets in my arms, and I look for somewhere to put her down so that she can move about on her own. The mistakes I am making as a novice godfather are growing increasingly obvious. I've been very selfish in bringing her to the hospital with me. I didn't even think to bring a blanket and toys to keep her occupied. I arranged everything so that I wouldn't need to carry around the bottle and lots of spare clothes, but I didn't think of the other things she might need. The only thing that occurs to me now is to put her on the bed beside Elsa, but I'd need a bit more space for that.

I spread my coat out in the sun and put Clara on it while I make a more comfortable space beside the inert body. I stop for a moment. Elsa looks so peaceful now, compared to how she looked a moment ago. Not a trace of the contorted face and grasping hands she had while her body was contracting.

There was one good thing about the spasm, even though I'd rather it hadn't happened: I saw her eyes for the first time. The pale blue shone out of them, even in the state she was in. I think for a minute and then remember where I've seen that colour before – in the photo on the door. The blue of the ice she was walking on.

Before seeing that photo I would never have believed that ice could be so blue. As far as I was concerned ice was either white, like the frost from the freezer, or transparent, if it started to melt, or if it was in cubes in a drink. My frame of ice references is fairly restricted, in fact. The only blue ice I'd seen was the fluorescent blueberry-flavoured slush that you drink, and I thought that was absolutely vile.

In that photo I can see what majesty the planet is capable of producing. It surprises me because, working in ecology, I've already done case studies on sea ice and glaciers. But I'm not a specialist in the area, so my experience is limited to the first two years I spent studying general ecology. Since then I've concentrated on wind power and other things. Elsa has brought me back to earth. Well, back to ice.

I sigh and shake my head. I came across this girl by accident ten days ago, and now my whole world seems to revolve around her. I have no desire to see that glacial blue again right now, but I do want to see it again one day. And she's not necessarily going to spend years longer in the coma, just because the doctor didn't want to answer my question. He might even have been worried about telling me that there would be another three months to wait. Three months could seem a long time to some people; not to me.

He did give me some other pretty significant information. Elsa can survive for two hours without electrical support. I had already understood from the other day that many of the contraptions she was attached to were different types of monitor, but I didn't know that it would be possible to unplug them all for a little while without causing any trouble.

Now I know that, I feel better.

I lean over her and pick up the tube of her artificial respirator. I tremble at the thought of doing something with irrevocable consequences. But I had the assurance five minutes ago that, for a certain length of time, it would have no effect. I grit my teeth and close my eyes. Click. I've just pulled out the transparent respirator tube.

The reassuring beep still sounds on the monitor beside her. I don't dare do anything to the machine, which is now pumping into fresh air. I'm sure the hospital staff have ways of surveying all this equipment from a distance. I lean over the bed and move aside the infusion tube, and unclip two or three others, so that I can move Elsa across the bed more easily. Finally I have my hand on the pulse monitor. It's the only thing that stands between this relative calm, and all the nurses racing in on 'red alert'.

I slide my hand underneath Elsa's body. I know I'm no stronger than I was the last time I came, but today I've decided that I'll manage it, even if it gives me an elbow cramp. I summon up all my manly strength in preparation for the lift, at the same time as detaching the monitor on her finger. My other hand goes around her waist and, with a pitiable groan, I manage to move her about twenty centimetres across the bed.

In a rush of adrenaline I hastily re-attach the pulse monitor to her finger and plug in all the other apparatus that I've taken out. I also rearrange the other wires that have moved. Perfect: Elsa is just the same as she was a few moments ago, but a bit further over. The less perfect thing is the painful cramp which has taken hold just under my shoulder blades, but it was worth it.

I turn to glance at Clara. She is lying on her back as I left her; her little eyes are beginning to close. The wool lining of my coat must be like a warm, downy mattress. I imagine myself in her place and my eyes feel a little heavier too.

I pick up Clara and put her on the bed beside Elsa. She wriggles happily; this spot must be much cosier than a coat on the hard floor. I take off my shoes as quickly as possible and sit down on the end of the bed to survey the scene.

I know that Gaëlle and Julien sometimes sleep on their backs with Clara on her front on their chests, but I'm not sure that will work in such a tight space. I'll put myself on one side, with Clara between Elsa and I. Then there won't be any risk of her falling.

The key is not to fall asleep but, even though I feel a bit sleepier every time I see a yawn from my goddaughter, I know that I'll stay alert to keep an eye on her. I place myself on the very edge of the mattress, to leave her as much space as possible, but I don't actually think she would notice if I got a bit closer. Her unmoving hands tell me that she is fast asleep.

My gaze lands on the person lying just behind her. Her right arm is resting at a strange angle and I realise that I must have draped it across her stomach when I moved her. I pick it up very gently, as though I might wake her, and put it down by her side. Clara is next to her though and, in spite of all my efforts, I am forced to leave the inanimate arm in contact with her. She doesn't seem bothered and I curl myself around the sleeping baby to make a sort of cocoon. My knees touch Elsa's legs, and my forehead touches her shoulder.

This close the smell of jasmine, which seems always to emanate from her, is stronger. Or perhaps the smell comes from the sheets? I close my eyes for a moment and it makes me want to cry. A sob escapes before I have a chance to hold it back. It feels like letting go of a ball of worry.

I am a disgrace. Shameful. I have to be lying on a hospital bed beside a woman in a coma and a sleeping baby before I can feel any real emotion. I did cry when I was with Julien last week, but that's not the same. The two people with me in this room are never going to tell anyone that I've cried, or how pathetic my whimpers are. Here I can let myself go.

So I cry and cry. I cry for my arrogance, my weakness, for my desperation. I cry about not being able to talk to my brother. I cry about my jealousy of Gaëlle and Julien, of their harmonious relationship, and their perfect family. I dream of being in their place, and instead I bring their daughter with me to this hospital, and feel self-conscious every time a woman looks at me.

Suddenly I feel cold, but I know that it's only in my mind. I'm not actually cold, but I wish someone's arms were around me. Not my mother's, not Julien's, and certainly not my brother's. No, the only arms that could reassure me today are the inert ones lying a few centimetres away from me. And I realise that I need these arms for the simple reason that I can't have them at the moment, and that if I decide I would like them to comfort me one day, I will have to fight for them. Really fight – probably for the first time in my life.

Things have always come easily to me. Passing exams, success in my studies; I've always moved relatively smoothly from one stage of my life to the next, finding a partner, living together. Even with Cindy, it was easy. And the breakup was relatively easy too, when I really think about it, because she gave me so many reasons to hate her. The whole thing came to a quick and definitive conclusion. It's the secondary effects that have been less straightforward, and I have let myself be overwhelmed by them. I made a good start by finding a new place to live, but I haven't really made any progress since then. And then there was my brother's accident. The time has come to dig myself out of this.

The time has come to dig *her* out of this.

My sobs break off as quickly as they began. There's my decision: I'm going to fight. For myself, and for Elsa. I want her to wake up, and *I* want to wake up as well. Two objectives that run parallel to each other, two life rafts. I will play the conscious part for us both, and she will do the . . . well . . . I'm not quite sure which part she can play, but I need to believe that she will do something.

The last tears dry as I start to smile.

I feel a warmth beneath my fingers, then I lower my eyes and discover that it is Elsa's arm I am holding.

I need to calm down.

No, I am calm. I need to think this through properly. Julien was right.

I'm in love with a girl who's in a coma.

And for the moment, this seems like the most sensible thing that has ever happened to me.

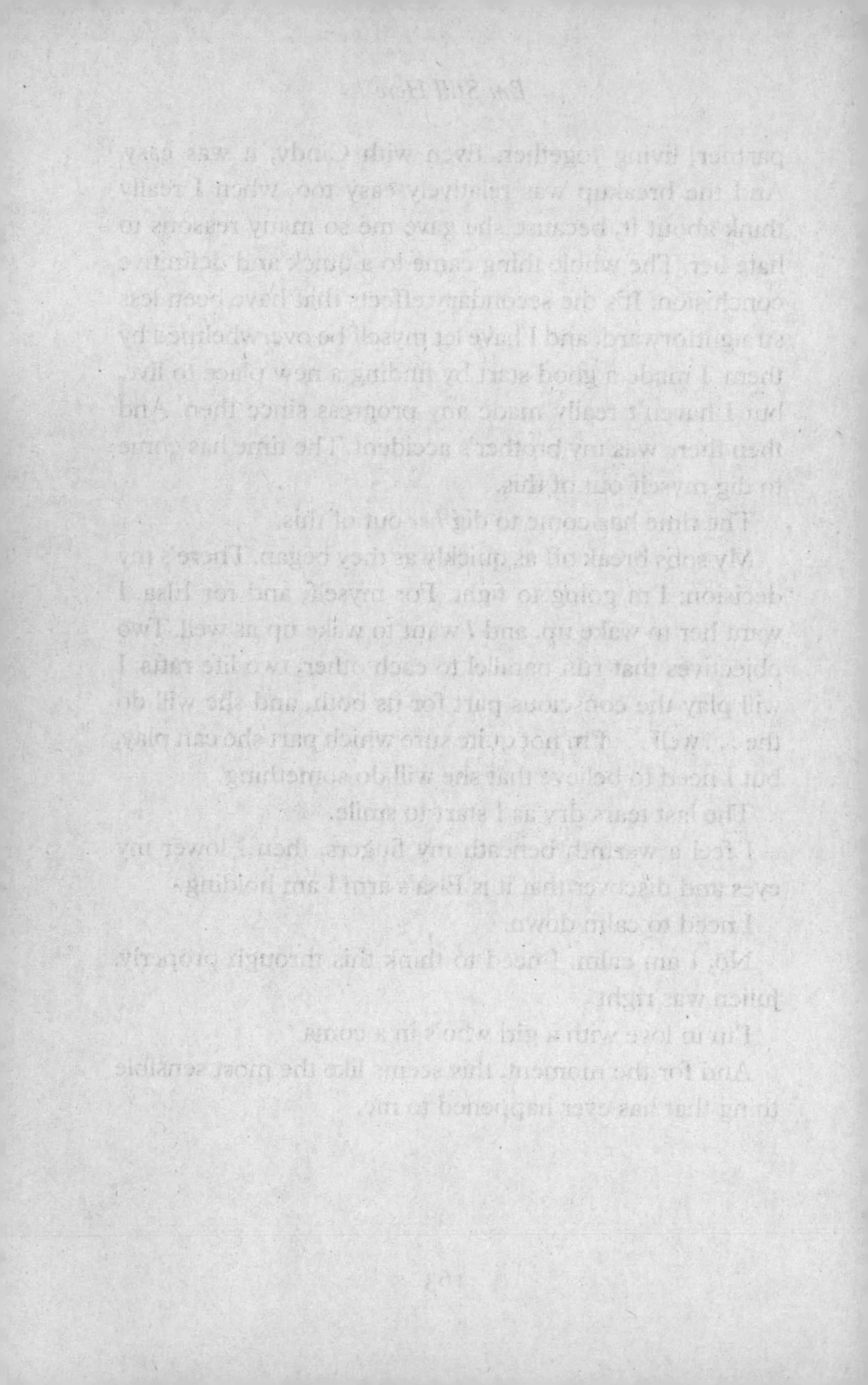

17

Elsa

This is too delicious. I am lying beside a rainbow and a golden snowflake. All the colours shine in front of my closed eyes, different shades, full of sparks and twinklings which gleam brightly but still effuse a gentle quality. I think the baby has fallen asleep, her breathing is so calm and smooth. Thibault's breathing sounds as though he is still awake. My breathing sounds as though . . .

My breathing sounds as though Thibault hasn't connected my respirator properly.

I followed each of his movements. I couldn't quite match every click with its monitor, but I know the respirator sound well. And now I can hear a light whistling sound. The tube passes just below my ear and there's definitely a stream of oxygen escaping out into my room. There's no need to panic, if indeed panicking is something I am able to do. There should be enough air getting into my lungs for me to breathe. No need to be frightened.

Fear . . . I really don't want to feel that dreadful fear again, so I focus my attention on the thing I do now whenever Thibault is present.

I want to turn my head and open my eyes.

I want to turn my head and open my eyes.

I want to turn my head and open my eyes.

Suddenly something interrupts my repetition. Warmth. Softness. Contact. It's gone again, I must have imagined it.

I want to turn my head and open my eyes.

I want to turn my head and open my eyes.

Softness again.

Don't be silly, Elsa, what could you possibly be feeling?

I want to turn my head and open my eyes.

Warmth. Localised.

Localised? But where?

Gone.

But I didn't imagine it. I know because a purple spot appeared in front of my eyes at the moment I felt the warmth.

Felt . . . how can I be sure that I didn't imagine it? With all my visualisation exercises, how can I tell the difference between real and imagined?

I leave my questioning, and I decide that it must have been real. After all, Maria the cleaning lady seemed to think she heard me singing the other day. Well . . . singing might be a slight exaggeration. I probably just exhaled more heavily than normal. But she was so convinced. And with that music going through my head, I wanted to believe that I had finally managed to emit a signal to the outside world.

That makes me want to laugh. I am like an extra-terrestrial trying to make contact with the inhabitants of Earth. An extraterrestrial who, for now, is only able to communicate in colours. And again, 'communicate' is a strong word. Normally communication works both ways. Whereas in this case it's only—

Sudden warmth.

Electric surge.

The beeps on the pulse monitor get faster and shorter, then they calm down after a moment. Next to me Thibault moves. I think he must be trying to look at the screen which shows the reading of my pulse. He pauses, as though he is trying to understand, or as though he is waiting for something. He must change his mind or be satisfied that things are normal, because the next sound indicates that he's stretching out again. At least halfway.

Then again, I could be wrong. But I don't see why he would be sitting up. Usually, when he is next to me, he spends some time rearranging himself, like a cat looking for a place to sit. I haven't heard any of that happening. It doesn't matter; he must be thinking, or watching Clara or something. Who cares? He is here, that's what counts. Because I've got work to do and I know that I'm more likely to succeed when Thibault is around.

I want to turn my head and open my eyes.

I want to turn my head and open my eyes.

Warmth and contact.

On the arm.

The beep on my left sounds four times quickly and then stabilises again.

'What the hell is going on?'

Even if he only said that very quietly, it's clear that Thibault is worried. After all, he's the one who moved me, which could have had any kind of effect. And he did reconnect my respirator wrong, although he doesn't know that. But I don't think the accelerated beating of my heart has anything to do with the respirator at the moment.

I managed to identify that the warmth was in my arm.

I felt. I really felt. Not in my imagination this time, I'm certain. For a few moments, my brain communicated with my arm. I don't actually know which one, left or right. But I felt it.

And I want to feel it again.

I thirst for contact, like a dependence or an addiction so severe that you would need several months of rehabilitation to get over it. An insatiable thirst which could make my throat tighten, could haunt my dreams, and make me tremble all the way to my fingertips.

My wish is granted a few breaths later.

I feel something again.

Warmth, softness, contact.

In the right arm this time, I'm certain. I know that I can't move it. I don't even need to try. But I concentrate on the little sensory influxes to try and associate them with memories. After what must be quite a long time, I can distinguish two separate areas of warmth, contact, softness. One of them is still. The other one moves. At least, that's what it feels like.

This is crazy . . . I can't feel my legs, or my hands, or anything else, but I can isolate two very specific areas of my body which must add up to the size of a couple of postage stamps.

A sudden break in the rhythm of the beep from the monitor on my right makes me abandon these reflections. It's my turn to wonder what's going on. I don't understand anything else. I can't feel anything else. In fact, I can still feel one of the zones of contact, the immobile one. But the place where the sensation was moving is gone. I wish I had even a tiny idea what was going on.

The noises suddenly fade away. It's almost as though my brain has voluntarily muffled the noises in order to concentrate on something else. But on what?

I hear that electronic wailing beep in the distance, the sound which always panics the doctors, and I wonder why no one has burst into my room yet. But my notion of time is horribly confused; I can't tell if my pulse has been disturbed for a second or for an hour.

This is the first time that my hearing has failed me. Maybe the respirator really was necessary. Perhaps these are my last moments of consciousness. I want to grit my teeth and fight to get my senses back. Or, at least, my hearing. I really want to understand what's going on.

Everything is muddling together in my head. Colours, textures, thoughts. I can't tell if two days have passed or only a few minutes . . .

Gradually, I get back to normal. I hear the beep regulate itself, I hear the motor on the respirator, I hear the flow of air through the tube, I hear Thibault, sobbing.

I was aware of that sound earlier. Heavy, dark, full of a bitterness which corresponds to the grey shades which pass in front of my eyes. The colour is nothing like the colour of earlier. It's strange, like a mixture of sadness and joy. Incomprehensible. So I stop trying to analyse it.

I hear my body take a deep breath.

That is surprising, but perhaps after such excitement my body needs to refuel itself. I still don't understand why, though.

Why . . . that seems to be the only thing I can ask myself today.

18

Thibault

I couldn't resist. I kissed her.

I thought she would feel cold. My first mistake.

I thought she would feel stiff. My second mistake.

Of course, she didn't exactly respond to my kiss, but she felt supple. Supple enough that it was like kissing someone who was asleep. The sort of kiss you might give someone in the middle of the night, maybe to wake them up. Or maybe to make sure they are still there, in one of those moments when the night seems to have given everything a different tint. It might just be a sentimental thing, or it might be physical, or maybe a mixture of the two – I can't remember the last time I shared that kind of moment with someone.

But there it is, I don't know what came over me.

Some people might say something like: 'It was stronger than I was.' I can't stand that expression. I'd say . . .

It was inevitable.

I kissed her.

I bite my knuckle to release the tension. I've been back at Gaëlle and Julien's for two hours and I still feel over-excited. It must be the adrenaline, or maybe it's the hormones that shoot around your system when you have that kind of contact with someone. I was bathed in a sort of euphoria earlier, I got back to the apartment almost on autopilot. How absurdly we behave when we're in love . . .

A cry from Clara brings me back down to earth. It must be time for me to get her evening bottle ready.

When I got in I put the television on, out of habit, but I've kept the volume very low. I suppose it's for the company, or as a distraction. But it hasn't worked. Not even Clara can take my mind off this afternoon.

When the bottle's ready, I lie her across me and she feeds happily. My eyes wander around the living room and eventually land on their target. The pushchair manual. I do have a project for tomorrow, and I need to learn how to unfold this stupid contraption. But another book on the coffee table catches my attention.

It's strange that I even saw it, it's so well hidden amongst the magazines. It was me who left it there the last time, deliberately stashed so that I would forget it when I left. I hesitate for a minute. I wonder why Julien really bought me this book, even as he was telling me all week to be careful of what I thought and felt for Elsa. Perhaps he thought it would deter me from going to visit her. Either that or he's trying to advance my medical education. I have my doubts about that theory, though.

I don't move, on the cusp of a decision until Clara finishes her bottle. The book and I seem to be staring each other down. I look over at it as though I might be able to make it levitate towards me, and in return it dares me to come over and pick it up. Luckily for the book, it wins some extra time while I go and put Clara to bed. But at about nine o'clock, after dinner and a shower, I come in ready to tackle it, like a soldier who's been ritually prepared for battle.

I skip most of the preface. It seems like a fairly good summary, but I only skim it to get to the introduction. Five seconds later, I have already worked my way through about ten pages and I feel as though I'm getting to the heart of the matter.

The explanations begin quite simply, with only a few technical phrases. But the language soon gets more scientific. When I eventually lift my head out of the book to look at the clock, it is . . . ten past nine. No, that's impossible – I feel as though I've been wrestling with this thing for several hours. I think perhaps it belongs under the magazines for now. I know when I've been beaten.

There's also a part of me that doesn't actually want to know when a person who's in a coma starts running out of chances to wake up.

I have no idea what state Elsa is in, and nobody seems to want to tell me. And I realise that I prefer it that way. Staying in the dark, living in ignorance, means that I can keep on hoping. And hope is what keeps me going on a day like today.

At nine fifteen, I pick up the pushchair instructions and creep back into Clara's room to retrieve the object of my disaffection. In the living room I push aside the coffee table so that I've got a bit more room to manoeuvre. The movements that follow resemble an extremely bad ballet. I turn into a terrible dancer, the unskilled partner of a reluctant pushchair who refuses to bend, or unbend rather, to any of my requirements. It's a sad excuse for a duet.

I eventually retire from the spectacle, victorious, at ten o'clock, leaving the pushchair open in the hallway. Although I have folded and unfolded it at least five times in a row to make sure that I have learned how it's done, I'm still a little frightened of not being able to do it again in the morning.

I get everything ready for Clara, who will wake me up in the middle of the night, and then I lie myself carefully out on the bed. The battle with the pushchair must have tired me out more than I realised, because I am asleep quickly. At four in the morning, a foggy-minded creature gives the baby her bottle before plunging back into a deep sleep.

The alarm goes off at seven. Or, rather, my phone vibrates at seven. I get up quickly so as not to disturb Clara.

It's funny how much a situation can remind you of another completely separate one. I remember waking up quietly like this for several years, so as not to disturb Cindy, who always slept for a quarter of an hour longer than me. I would creep out and get her breakfast ready, at first out of love, and later out of habit. On reflection, I think she only thanked me for doing this during the first few weeks. I didn't mind though, I was in love, and later I was used to it. Today, I'm just devoted to my miraculous little companion. And I know that Clara isn't going to abandon me.

I get everything organised, so that when she wakes up I am completely ready to look after her. I wrap her up in plenty of clothes to make sure she's warm enough, as Gaëlle instructed. I also remember to look for the pink hat I gave her when she was born. I find it put neatly away with the rest of her 'outings clothes', as Julien calls them, which seems appropriate as it is an outing that I have in mind. A bit of a strange one, though. It will be a new experience for my goddaughter. And a new experience for me as well. I've never been jogging with a pushchair. I know that the model of pushchair Julien has is suitable for jogging. Still, I feel a little apprehensive, although I think it's more excitement than anxiety. For the first time since the beginning of December, I don't look quite so much like a cosmonaut. My jacket stays on the dresser when I close the door behind me.

Getting into the lift with the buggy is not as complicated as I had thought, unlike the seemingly simple task of getting out of the building. At nine on a Sunday morning there aren't many people around to hold the door open – none in fact. I instruct Clara to cover her ears while I swear profusely at the possibility that, after all this preparation, we may not even make it out of the door. When we do eventually get outside, I feel instantly revitalised.

I don't fully comprehend my mixture of feelings, but I enjoy the simple fact of seeing the rays of sunlight filter through the clouds. Supposedly, it's going to rain, but I've brought the plastic covering for the pushchair anyway. I don't want Clara to get cold.

I head towards the park at a good pace. After a few hundred metres I have settled into the running shoes that I've borrowed from Julien. If the pushchair is as well adapted to jogging as I seem to be, this is going to be more fun than I expected. As soon as we arrive at the paved walkways that criss-cross through the park, I gather speed. I find myself trotting along behind it quite awkwardly at first, and then with greater assurance as we make our way around the park. In the pushchair, Clara is more alert than ever. The new experience delights her. I was sceptical about attempting this a few days ago, but now that I'm here I am fully convinced. In my head I even start planning for future sessions. I'll have to talk to Julien about it, but perhaps we could go running like this, together, from time to time. I even wonder if Gaëlle would enjoy it too.

By about ten o'clock the park has more people in it, but still fewer than I had imagined. The sun is beginning to hide behind the clouds, so I head back to the apartment and get there just in the nick of time, running for the last part as the rain begins to fall.

I arrive soaked, both with sweat and with rain, but first I have to look after the sleeping beauty in the pushchair. I undress her and change her, after which she refuses categorically to let me put her down. We wander into the living room to play, but my mood sinks as the light drains from the sky. It's not even midday yet, and you'd think that night was falling. It looks strangely like what my brother was watching from his wheelchair yesterday afternoon.

When a ray of sunlight pierces the clouds, I go to the window to try and recapture the mood of our outing this morning. But nothing comes back. It's as though my body has lost its memory.

In the distance rain is falling. There's just one little spot with sun shining onto it making a pale rainbow overhead. For some reason it reminds me of the indicator lights on a screen in that room at the hospital. I pick out the colours one by one and point them out to Clara, though I know she won't remember, as I will, this particular Sunday in which her soon-to-be godfather tried to help her understand this miracle.

I sigh as I gaze at the rainbow. I feel apathetic again. It's as though I'm imitating my brother's new attitude. Clara must notice because she starts wriggling and wanting to be put down. I put her into her bed and go back to the window, beckoned by it somehow.

The driving rain at the end of the rainbow looks like the state of my heart. I suddenly want to cry out in misery, but I know that I shouldn't. I've already cried enough. I've made my decisions. I hate storms, but this rainbow gives me some hope in spite of it.

Storms must be good for something.

19

Elsa

I can hear the repulsive sound of the languorous kiss that my sister and her boyfriend are currently engaged in. How dare she do that in my bedroom? She has never had to think about boys or how to behave around them; she's always just picked one from the long line of them that constantly follows her around.

If my ears don't deceive me, I think this boy may even have his hands up her shirt. She laughs, but obviously thinks better of whatever she was about to do, because the hungry lip noises eventually stop.

A mental sigh of relief. I was sick of listening to them kiss, yes, but I was also jealous. Not because my sister hasn't spoken to me as much as usual today, but because I haven't had any contact of that kind for what seems like an eternity.

When I woke up this morning I had lost all sense of time, but then Pauline and her companion arrived so I knew it must be Wednesday. I couldn't work out what the date was until she answered the phone. I think it's the tenth, but I'm not completely sure. At least I know that Christmas is in a couple of weeks. I wonder what exciting presents will be coming my way.

None, presumably.

What do you give a girl in a coma? Especially when she's just had her birthday. And when all the doctors want to unplug her.

I think back to Christmas last year. I was bored out of my mind, stuck at one of those interminable gatherings where you always see exactly the same people and eat exactly the same food. All I could think about was grabbing my skis and making a dash for it, to make the most of the one day of the year when there would be hardly anyone on the slopes, and no queue for the chair lifts. My mother told me off several times that day, I remember, for my lack of festive spirit. She said that I was being antisocial, but I dodged the criticism by complaining that I didn't understand how my sister had been allowed to bring a boyfriend she had only known for two weeks, when I hadn't been allowed to invite one of my oldest friends.

The friend I wanted to invite was Steve. My whole family already knew him, but they still said no. My father had hated him ever since he became my climbing buddy. And my mother ignored him as soon as she realised that he was only my climbing buddy, and nothing more. My sister . . .

I have no idea what my sister thought about it actually – for once I don't think she made any comment – but suddenly I have a feeling I'm about to find out. Outside my bedroom door I hear several people talking and one of them sounds like Steve. I am overcome with joy, truly overcome. Submerged in joy even, because my victory for this week has been that I am now able to perceive my emotions.

I can feel whatever is circulating in my blood. I feel the chemical messages running through me, bringing messages from my brain and later returning there, charged with new information. Disgust, followed by joy, are the two that I have experienced so far today. Yesterday it was grief and anger.

Yesterday's were because my consultant and Loris came to pay me a visit. In fact, they came to stand over me and talk about my situation. It was as though they needed me there, in front of them, to be better able to argue their cases for the relative hopelessness of my plight. The consultant gave the junior a massive bollocking when he learned that he had told my parents about the seizure on Saturday. Loris was defending himself by reminding his boss that it was correct procedure to let them know. The consultant insisted that, once the 'minus X' had been written in the notes, it was normal practice to overlook insignificant details. The seizure had just been a reflex, a message from the autonomic nervous system, and definitely not via my brain. I let some of the medical terms go over my head, even though I was curious to hear what the consultant's arguments were. When I came back to myself there was no one left in my room.

But now I find myself in the midst of five people, and they're making a monumental noise.

'Pauline!' squeals Rebecca. 'I hadn't realised you'd be here, how wonderful to see you. How are you?'

My sister's reply is enthusiastic. I can just imagine the look of suffering on her boyfriend's face, *in flagrante* one minute and then finding himself amongst three strangers the next. She introduces everyone. He emits a pained little grunt in place of a hello. I don't think he stays more than six seconds before making a beeline for the exit.

Steve and Alex snigger in the corner while Rebecca worries as usual.

'Do you think we frightened him off?'

'Oh relax, Rebecca!' answers my sister. 'He's just a bit wild. I haven't tamed him yet.'

'Judging by the way he had you round the waist a minute ago, "wild" is definitely the word,' laughs Alex.

'Alex!' shout both girls simultaneously.

'Oh, come on, we're allowed to laugh in here, aren't we?'

'I agree with Alex,' adds Steve.

'Uh . . . I'm sorry.'

Intriguing. That was definitely my sister's voice, but not a version of my sister's voice that I have ever heard before. It was an embarrassed murmur of an apology that didn't sound convincing at all, as though it was directed towards someone in particular. That really wasn't like her . . . Then suddenly, I understand.

My sister and Steve. Oh help . . . Can my sister actually be in love with Steve?

Now that this theory has crossed my mind, I wonder why I didn't think of it sooner. It's so obvious! Or maybe not – perhaps you have to be in a coma to pick up these signals. All these things I've never noticed. That must be why I could never quite put my finger on what my sister thought of him.

This idea gives me an opportunity to experience my newest feeling of the moment, compassion. Because I find myself hoping very strongly that my sister manages to show him how she feels. Maybe not in this hospital room though, please. Steve is not the sort to waste any time on small talk, not even with girls.

I think it's only with me that he has really tried to get in touch with his sensitive side and, unfortunately for him, it didn't work out romantically, even if sensitivity is a characteristic that I like in a man.

I paint a mental picture of Steve and my sister together. It makes me smile inside. I imagine smiling in real life.

'She looks happy today,' says Rebecca.

I know that she's talking about me because her footsteps come over to my bed. I want to scream with joy when I feel the contact of her hand on my left arm, my second victory since Thibault's visit.

'Well, I don't see why she should.' My sister's voice makes my blood run cold. New emotion: apprehension. I haven't reached fear yet. And, to tell the truth, it's the first time that I wish I couldn't feel anything at all.

'What are you saying, Pauline?' asks Steve.

'No, nothing.'

'Do you think we're going to let you leave it at that without an explanation?'

What was I saying, about Steve and sensitivity? They just don't go together.

'I'm not allowed to talk about it,' begins my sister.

'What do you mean, not allowed?'

'Because you're not family.'

Steve must be reaching boiling point. I think Rebecca moves closer to my sister.

'Pauline, you must know that, for Elsa, we are part of her family, even if we aren't actually related. You can't leave it at that, after what you've just said. What's going on?'

I silently thank Rebecca for her firm but gentle intervention. It is wonderful to hear someone speak about me as though I am still actually alive, and in such a tactful, sympathetic way. My beloved friends want an answer and they won't leave until they get it.

'Do you really need me to explain?'

My sister's voice breaks my heart. I think she's going to cry.

'She's not going to wake up, is that it?'

Steve's voice is as cold as the glaciers we used to walk on together. In my head his colours have just gone from red to the iciest blue I can imagine. Too much emotion for me. I almost want to duck out of this conversation.

'The doctors say not.'

The tone of my sister's voice indicates that she has concluded her explanation. Nobody speaks, at least not straight away.

Predictably, it is Alex who steps in first. 'Thank you, Pauline. I'm sure Elsa would have wanted you to tell us.'

'I have no idea what Elsa would have wanted, and now I don't think I ever will,' retorts my sister angrily.

'Calm down, Pauline. It won't do any good to get yourself in a state.'

'What do you mean, won't do any good? I'll get into any kind of state I want!'

I don't think I've ever heard my sister speak like that.

At that moment I hear the door handle squeak again. It's so quiet I can hear the breathing of all four of the people in the room. Is it the boyfriend coming back?

'Uh . . . It looks like I've come at a bad time.'

Thibault. My rainbow. He is going to have a challenge on his hands, dissipating the electric atmosphere in this room.

'Yes, it looks like it,' replies my sister. 'Who are *you*?'

'Calm down, Pauline.'

This time the instruction comes from Steve. I'm touched and surprised.

'Come with me,' he says.

'Where?' she practically spits.

'Outside. You need to breathe.'

I think he takes her arm and leads her out to the corridor. The door clicks behind them and a heavy silence takes over the room. It's exactly as I thought. Even with Steve and my sister outside, the storm rages on in here.

'Hello, you two . . .' says Thibault, coming over. 'It really seems like I've come at the wrong moment. Or have I done something I shouldn't have?'

I imagine my rainbow feeling awkward, and not knowing how to behave. That's how his voice sounds, anyway. I have more desire than ever to turn my head and open my eyes. I am so desperate to see him.

'No, it's just that Elsa's sister is a little bit . . . uncomfortable,' says Alex carefully.

'I wouldn't have called that uncomfortable,' says Thibault.

Nobody answers him. I hear him come over to me. I put all the working parts of my brain on full systems alert. By concentrating, I feel contact on my forehead, in my hair and on my cheek at the same time as I hear his hand pass over. I feel as though I could drift away, even drown, in his gentle warmth, vast as an ocean. But the sensation is so light and fragile, it's almost like a butterfly's wing moving.

Thibault's breathing is very close, as close as on the days when he has slept next to me.

'I won't stay today, Elsa,' he says, as quietly as possible. 'Lots of people have come to visit you, so I mustn't be selfish and try and keep you all to myself.'

Confused emotions. A chaotic mixture of jealousy, desire, sadness and something else that I can't quite identify.

I feel one thing clearly. Thibault kisses my cheek. It's like an explosion of flavours. I focus every bit of my brain, even the inactive parts, on what I can feel. I think I could describe the exact shape of his lips, the roundness of his mouth, every crease on that pink flesh that I dream of kissing.

More than ever I want to turn my head and open my eyes.

The warmth goes away before I manage it.

Instead of drowning in the contact, I am drowning in my own misery as I listen to Thibault say goodbye to Rebecca and Alex. He leaves the room and I am a world away again. Even my friends' voices don't bring me back to them. I do manage to catch a few words, but it's as though the sounds are muffled by clouds.

'Do you think we should talk to him? He seems so close to her now . . .'

'No, leave him. At least one person can still dream.'

20

Thibault

I look from my watch to the clock on the wall of my office and back again about every three minutes, as though one of them might have lied to me. It's been like this all day. I haven't turned a page of the file in front of me since I put it down there earlier. I'm not sure if I've even touched it, to tell the truth.

I know what's going on. I have a yearning that won't go away until tomorrow, because I didn't see her yesterday. Well, I did see her, but only for two minutes, and it took all the gentlemanliness I could muster not to stay and monopolise her for the whole hour as I had envisaged. I spent the time wandering through the corridors of the hospital, and passed back in front of room 52 several times. I also passed in front of my brother's room. My mother had left the door ajar to tempt me again.

Eventually I was tempted. I went into the room without saying anything. My mother was occupying the one uncomfortable chair left in the room for visitors. So I picked up a magazine and sat down on the floor in the corner. They tried to get me to talk but I didn't even raise my eyes towards them.

I listened to their conversation with one ear while skimming through the magazine, a compilation of wacky news articles, several weeks out of date. I didn't even notice when my mother went out. It was only when my brother cleared his throat that I lifted my eyes at last and noticed that we were alone. We stared at each other for a moment, in silence, before my brother spoke. He started with small talk and then launched into what was actually on his mind:

'Why do you never come and see me?'

'Do you need to ask?' I replied flatly.

'Well, no . . . not really,' he said with a sigh. 'You think I deserve whatever's coming to me. But I'll ask the question another way. What do you do all the time Mum's in here? Do you stay in the car?'

I closed the magazine, glanced at the door, and decided to tell him everything. Without pausing, I recounted my spells of despair in the stairwell, my angry rages, and then mistakenly walking into room 52 two weeks ago and meeting Elsa. I told him about all my moments of indecision, and also about the moment when I realised that I was in love with the girl in the coma. I also told him that I still couldn't get my head around the idea that my brother had killed two people, just because he'd been too pig-headed not to get behind the wheel drunk.

I let him have all the information at once, in whatever order it occurred to me, but he followed the story. At one moment I even thought I could see his eyes shining, but no, that was impossible.

'Are you still as angry with me now as you were at first?' he asked, after my monologue.

'I don't know what you mean.'

'I mean, what's made you come here now?'

'What do you mean?'

'I *mean* what are you doing in my room? Did your girlfriend not want to see you today?'

I leapt up and, in less than two seconds, was on top of him, my hands on his chest, my face a few inches from his.

'Don't you dare speak about her like that! You, of all people.'

My eyes held his for what seemed like a long time, until he looked away. What he said next gave me a shock.

'You really are in love.'

It wasn't said nastily or with any sense of mockery. He was envious. I couldn't understand what was going on. Especially when he continued to speak.

'You're really in love and I envy you. Not just the being in love, but being able to experience that kind of emotion. I've never really been serious or . . . profound, yeah, that's the word. I've never had any profound feelings about anyone. I don't know. Maybe I've been afraid they wouldn't love me back? Or maybe I just couldn't be bothered. Anyway, I realise that's pathetic now, and that maybe no one will ever love me back. But even realising it doesn't mean that I can actually *feel* any of the emotions I've realised I don't feel. I'm still in the same place I was before. Does that make sense, Thibault?'

I stayed still while he spoke, until I was sure he had finished. I was utterly taken aback. I didn't give my mother enough credit when she told me that my brother had been thinking about what had happened. Maybe I should have.

'You only need to try,' I said to him, going back to sit in my corner.

'I would like to,' he said, without elaborating.

'What are you waiting for?'

'I don't know.'

After that, his gaze wandered outside and he didn't speak until my mother came back in. He did look at me for several seconds when we were leaving. The strangest, most chaotic, mixed-up look I've ever seen. He had such a confusion of emotions in his eyes that I wondered how on earth he could tell me that he didn't feel anything. Then I nodded a goodbye, or perhaps it was meant to be encouragement, I don't know. His response was even more underplayed than mine, and we left it there.

In the car, my mother tried to find out what we had spoken about during her ten minutes' absence. I almost had the impression that she had left us alone on purpose. When I dropped her off, she wanted me to stay with her. For once, I said yes without hesitation. I wasn't going to ask Julien to come and keep me company again. With Clara's christening on Sunday, he'd probably got better things to do than administer advice to his pathetic best friend.

I've resisted calling Julien for the last three hours because I have a feeling that tonight is going to be hard and I'm saving myself until then. I don't want to go back to my mother's because I know there will be a mountain of questions. I don't feel like going out with my colleagues because that would probably elicit even more interrogation. I just want to see Elsa.

The Book activates in my head. It has stayed all day on page 100, the 'Blank Page'. And then it's as though there's a sudden gust of wind which blows the page over to 99: 'Do Whatever You Feel Like Doing'.

What is stopping me from going to see Elsa tonight? Visits are allowed every day, it's just that the hours vary. It's Thursday. That means 3 till 6 today. There's my answer. I finish at 6, so there's no way I can get there.

Yes. There is one way.

I don't even take the time to linger on page 54: 'Do Everything You Need to in Order to Succeed', before hurrying into my boss's office. In *The Book*, it didn't say what you need to do to succeed, it just said *everything*. I choose partial honesty – I don't have the time to invent anything else.

'I've got something very important to do. Can I leave early?'

My boss looks at me with suspicion. I've never asked for any favours or special treatment since I've worked here, but my rages with Cindy when we split up have marked my personal record with a big red cross.

'What is it that's so important?' he asks with a sigh.

'It's complicated,' I reply, hesitant.

'I have a feeling it's you who is complicated, Thibault.'

'That's entirely possible.'

My response makes him smile and I see that I have won this round.

'What does early mean?' he asks, watching me already on my way out of his office.

'Right now?' I call back, telling myself that I only risk refusal if I turn around politely.

'Go on then. Get out of here. Tomorrow, in at 7 though.'

I nod my head to say yes, and then race back to my desk to collect my things. My heart is pounding, either because of my victory, or because I'm running down the stairs, I don't know. I don't really care.

I'm only interested in one thing.

I'm going to see her.

21

Elsa

Christmas has come early. It's Thursday and Thibault is here.

He's already been in my room for a little while. He arrived, euphoric, and told me all about his strange day and even said that he had left work early to come and see me. I was slightly bewildered. I suppose because he hasn't really had this sort of conversation – if you can call it a conversation – with me before. His multi-coloured voice was full of glimmering shades, which all danced around until finally they settled into a luxurious velvety texture, and I couldn't take much in after that. I still don't really understand what's going on, to tell the truth, but it doesn't matter. I feel good, that's what counts.

In spite of the 'minus X' scrawled on the clipboard at the end of my bed, I feel good.

What's more, it seems that Thibault is the only person unaware of the 'minus X' spanner in the works. That might be why I start to feel better when he's here, and why my senses come back in his presence. I love my family and my friends, of course, but . . . Thibault is the one I actually want to wake up for. There, I've said it.

Now it just seems normal that he is lying here next to me. He has reconnected my respirator badly, the same as last time, which will provoke grumblings from the nurse when she realises. At the moment she thinks the tube is sliding out by itself. She would never dream that there was someone coming in here and disconnecting it regularly on purpose.

I think Thibault is getting more used to moving me as well. Either that or he's been working out. But it's only been a few days so such a marked improvement would be surprising. I'm pretty sure that today he has pushed me all the way to the very edge of my bed, because I heard him sigh with contentment as he stretched out on the mattress. I don't think he's asleep yet though.

'Elsa . . .'

He's definitely not asleep. Or he's sleep-talking. But that voice sounded pretty wide awake.

'Elsa . . .'

I could shiver, I'm so desperate to answer him. His name has passed through my head more times in the past two weeks than any other thought over the last two months. It's the only thing I know for certain about him, his name. As for what he looks like, or anything else about him, I can only imagine.

In these hours of solitude I've had plenty of time to think about which senses I miss the most. At first, I was sure that sight was the most important one but, being isolated with only my ears for all this time, I've come to the conclusion that to be able to hear is a very great gift. I would love to know what Thibault smells like though.

As I am thinking this, the little beep next to me jumps about for several seconds, so I return to my mental exercises. But no mental exercise is as effective as having him lie beside me. And today, more than ever, I yearn to see his face, the colour of his eyes, to see the hands that sent me those electric shocks.

I would like to know what he feels like; if he uses aftershave; to recognise the smell of his skin. I would like to touch his body with mine from head to toe.

I leave the sense of taste aside for now, because the pulse monitor races too dramatically whenever I linger on it. Every time I have imagined kissing Thibault, bringing back the memory of his lips on my cheek, the nurse has rushed in. When that happened for the fourth time in less than half a day, the doctor on duty told them to stop interrupting him with it. He said that he would call his colleague, my consultant, to suggest putting me back through the scanner. But then he saw the 'minus X' in my notes and told the nurse to forget about what he'd just said.

This episode gave me a brief hope that I had a chance of showing the world that I was still here. Except I'm being regulated by such basic monitors that not one of them records any sign of cerebral activity. But I am alive!

If only I could scream out. I am alive!

'Elsa . . . when do you plan on waking up?'

Thibault's voice makes me want to cry. I can even feel my tear ducts trying to spring into action. It seems crazy to be able to sense where they are. I don't suppose it would be seen as any great victory if I woke up and declared proudly that I can locate and feel my tear ducts, but to me it's heavenly to be aware of the different parts of my body. To feel anything at all is another step on the road to movement. That's a little mantra I have invented for myself. My brain is capable of receiving information. Now I just wish that it could also send it.

I'd also like to be able to answer Thibault's question. But the fact that I don't have the answer makes my spirits plunge again. I know that it'll take more time for me to wake up. But I don't *have* time. The 'minus X' on my clipboard turns 'perhaps soon' into 'I'm racing against an unspecified countdown'. And even if I hope that this unspecified countdown is as long as possible, I know that it won't be infinite. Making this decision must be eating away at my parents. They haven't been in here since their unpleasant exchange with the doctor, so I know they must be thinking about it. And, in their place, if I knew that I had to finally reach the 'yes' conclusion, I don't think I'd want to drag it out too long.

'I want you to wake up.'

These words, in the sweetest whisper I have ever heard, remove me from any negative thoughts. I'm torn between the natural, sarcastic response: 'Yes, me too, funnily enough, Thibault!' and an emotionally charged: 'Thank you'. I imagine myself saying either one or the other. My body seems to understand this desire, because I hear myself sigh. I can almost feel my diaphragm shift inside my abdomen, even. More progress. If only Thibault could be nearby at all times.

I imagine him curled up here every hour of the day and night, breathing, shimmering, always here. I think again of his lips on my cheek. My heartbeat speeds up on the monitor, but not alarmingly. My thoughts, left unattended, go to the thing that I have forbidden myself to think about for some time, but I can't help it. The beep accelerates again and I marshal my brain to control it. I suppose it works.

After that my imagination goes completely off the rails. Completely.

And then everything coagulates.

A sensation goes all the way up my legs.

I'm cold.

'Elsa. You've got to wake up, and it looks as though you're going to have to put your back into it!'

His mocking tone surprises me as much as the cold sensation. What is he talking about?

'I've just allowed myself to take a peek at your legs. I hope you're not cross. I lifted the bottom of the cover. Nothing inappropriate, I only saw from your ankles to your knees. I was just wondering what they were like.'

I want to laugh. He's interested in the shape of my legs!

'I suppose I wanted to see what it really was, this alpinism. Hearing about it all, I imagined you to be incredibly muscular! But, my gorgeous girl, you're going to have some work to do on those spindly legs when you wake up!'

Once again, I want to laugh out loud, and to tell Thibault that I'll do whatever he thinks is necessary when I wake up, and that for the moment I don't care if my calves look like tree trunks or like twigs. I don't care! I'm cold, Thibault! I'm cold! Do you understand?

'I'm in love with you, Elsa.'

One. Two. Three. Beeeeeeeeeeep!

The pulse monitor lets out an almighty screech as my whole chest stiffens. The muscles in my neck tense suddenly, my head falls lightly backwards. My shoulders drop, my back arches, my breath stops. And then I fall back down.

My entire body is tingling, like an aftertaste, or should I say an after-feeling.

For a whole second, I was conscious of my entire body. Say it again, Thibault, I beg of you. I want to be me again.

'Elsa . . . I . . . I think you just heard what I said.'

Yes, I heard you, Thibault! Of course I did! I've been hearing you for two weeks! And I'd like to hear you say it again and again. To wake me up, to reassure me, just for the pleasure of knowing.

Knowing that someone in the world still believes in me.

But instead I hear a great noise of sheets moving and the weight of a body disengaging itself from the mattress. I hear my own body moved and put back into the middle of the bed. Then Thibault puts on his shoes and outer clothes. I know the ritual by heart. The sweater, the jacket, the zipping up, the scarf, the gloves, the hat in the pocket and a hand through the hair.

His weight on the edge of my bed.

'I know you can hear me, Elsa.'

His lips against my cheek. The pulse monitor beeps with the contact.

'You keep proving it to me.'

At that moment, I hear running footsteps outside my door, but they pass my room without stopping. It seems to remind Thibault of what he was preparing to do.

'See you tomorrow . . .'

Another kiss and he's gone.

My brain has stored away more information than ever. Now, to work.

22

Thibault

'Move!'

I am flattened against the wall of the corridor as soon as I leave Elsa's room, the panic in the nurse's voice enough to assure me that there is no time for politeness. I don't know what's going on, but the fifth floor is hopping. Nurses and doctors are running around in what I'm sure is an organised manner, but it looks like chaos to me. Something must have happened, and I really don't care.

My mind is elsewhere, floating somewhere between my heart and my body. I've never made a declaration of love in these circumstances before. In fact, I defy anyone to have made a declaration of love in these circumstances.

I take the stairs because the lifts are caught up with whatever emergency has set the ward into panic. When I arrive on the ground floor, the agitation seems to have spread down there as well. I leave the building, staying close to the walls so as not to get in the way of the members of staff hurrying outside. I notice a group of medics about thirty metres away. They must have something to do with the chaos inside.

I get into my car, my thoughts still hovering on the fifth floor around the frail body in room 52. The body I would like to have held in my arms. But when I saw those legs, so thin and fragile after their months of immobility, I recognised the selfishness of my desire and contented myself with sitting on the edge of the bed. I was worried I might break her.

I arrive back at mine twenty minutes later, without really having noticed the journey home. I sit on the sofa in a daze, my only movements automatic and habitual ones. As I sip my pineapple juice, the reality creeps over me slowly: I am in love with someone, and that someone heard me tell them so.

I sigh deeply and bite my lip to suppress an enormous smile. If I told anyone about this they would think I was crazy. I file away that thought, telling myself that I would feel like this whether I had met her before the coma or not.

The phone rings, removing me from the sofa and from my daydream.

'Hello?' I say, yawning.

'You're tired already?'

'Julien . . . am I not even allowed to yawn any more?'

'Not when I'm talking to you!'

'Fine, what do you want?'

He launches into a tirade of questions, almost certainly prepared for him by his wife, on the subject of Clara's christening. Have I thought properly about something-or-other, I mustn't forget about such-and-such, I must do this-that-and-the-other during the ceremony, and so on.

'I remember everything, don't worry! What is Gaëlle trying to do here, another godfather test? Was my Clara weekend not enough?'

'Yes, yes, you looked after her perfectly. Gaëlle is very pleased with you.'

'So . . .?'

'I'm just trying to calm things down a bit.'

Now I am surprised. Julien, the steadiest, most level-headed person I know is anxious?

'What's going on?' I ask.

'Oh, you know, getting the christening organised, things are a bit on edge, with Gaëlle.' His tone makes me hesitate.

'Julien . . . what are you actually saying?'

'Do you have any time this evening?'

'Of course I do! But what's going on?'

He is starting to make me anxious now.

'Oh, nothing serious, don't worry!'

'So what then?'

'I've just got something to tell you. Could we meet at the pub? Or at yours?'

'Yes, perfect! But are you sure you're OK?'

'Certain. See you in a minute.'

He hangs up. I'm perplexed, but I abandon the idea of calling him again to find out what's going on. He'll be here in a minute; I should just be patient.

I look around my apartment. I didn't notice when I got back earlier, when I was only half paying attention to what I was doing, but my living room is a pigsty.

I spend the next half-hour before he arrives tidying up, and then I look at what I've got to offer him when he gets here. The answer is clear: pineapple juice, or pineapple juice. But it's too late to do anything about it now. I'm sure he'll forgive me.

The intercom sounds. I open the door and wait for him to come up. When he gets up here a minute later, I scan his face for the reason for this sudden visit.

He comes in quickly, takes off his shoes and collapses onto my sofa.

I show him the juice bottle without saying a word and he nods. Neither of us has spoken since the exchange on the intercom. I sit down opposite and scrutinise him. It makes me laugh because it's usually the other way round.

'Why are you laughing?' he asks me.

'It's usually you waiting for me to speak these days. This time I'm waiting for you to open your mouth.'

Julien nods his head and I see him smile. Then he stops himself, taps his right hand with his left, to show that he is ticking himself off, and takes a deep breath.

'Gaëlle is pregnant.'

In a fraction of a second I experience a whole range of emotions. Happy for him, jealous of him, pleased that Clara will have a baby brother or sister, concerned about how they will fit another child into their tiny apartment, and I understand Julien's urge to 'calm things down', as he said on the phone. I try to sum all this up in one word.

'Amazing!'

Julien looks me in the eye and at last I see his face light up.

'I know!'

I get up to give him a hug of congratulations. I can sense his emotion at the prospect of becoming a father for the second time. I think he may even shed a tear – a tear of joy, naturally.

'Are *you* OK?' he asks me, sitting back down on the sofa.

'With news like that? Of course!'

'Yes, but . . .'

I understand his twinges of unease. He knows that I love children. Everyone knows it now. And he also knows that the fact that I'm still nowhere near having any is starting to bother me.

'It's fine, Julien. Don't be ridiculous. I'll find someone when the time's right.'

'It's quite something,' he says, sincerely.

'Yup, I know. But why were you so worried?'

I prefer to turn the conversation back towards him; I don't want to talk about the situation with Elsa.

'Well, that's what was worrying me,' he admits.

'What?'

'You.'

'Me?'

'Telling you about it.'

I would have burst into tears if I didn't feel that manly behaviour was called for in a situation like this. I let go that night in the street outside the pub, but this time I hold myself back.

'Julien, really mate, I love you but you can stop torturing yourself about this. Yes, I'm a bit jealous of your miraculous and perfect family, but I'll have one of my own one day, so you don't need to worry, OK?'

Julien seems to be checking my smile, in case I'm concealing something in it.

Apparently he doesn't find anything. He nods his head and I smile at him, amused. We both start laughing just as my phone starts ringing again.

'I'll be right back,' I say, still laughing.

I answer without checking to see who the call is from, smiling down the phone, still delighted by Julien's news. I turn serious as soon as I hear the tone of the person at the other end of the line. I can't quite make out where I recognise the voice from, but something tells me that it's not a courtesy call.

'Monsieur Gramont?'

'Speaking.'

'Good evening. I'm calling from the Rosalines Hospital.

My heart stops. The nurse's voice disappears into the fog that clouds my brain as it runs through all the possible reasons there could be for a call like this. The first person who comes to mind is Elsa. But I don't know why the hospital would be contacting me about her.

'Hello, Monsieur Gramont? Are you there?'

'Yes . . . sorry. I didn't hear you. Could you say that again, please?'

'I said that I'm calling because I couldn't get hold of the other contact, Madame Gramont. I think that's your mother, isn't it?'

'Yes. What's going on?'

'I . . . I'm very sorry to have to tell you over the phone, but . . . your brother is dead. He jumped out of his bedroom window about an hour ago. We tried to resuscitate him, but without success. I'm sorry. Everyone is sure that it was suicide. I really am sorry. You . . . you need to come to the hospital to . . . for some papers and to . . . well, you know.'

If she says sorry again I swear I'll hang up.

'Monsieur Gramont?'

I am liquefying. I feel terribly cold. Even though my mind has emptied itself, I somehow manage to answer her.

'I'll be there in thirty minutes with Madame Gramont.'

I hang up without giving her the chance to say anything else. I had moved out of the way, from habit, when I answered the phone, but now Julien comes over to me.

'Thibault? What's happened?'

At first I stay facing the window and then slowly I turn around, my manly exterior about to shatter into a thousand pieces.

'It's Sylvain . . .'

Julien knows immediately, I don't know how. Or perhaps he just knows that something important has happened.

'Do we need to go to the hospital?'

'I need to get my mother.'

'From hers?'

I nod, unable to say anything else. Julien moves around me while I stay rooted to the spot. He passes me my shoes and my cosmonaut jacket. I don't know how I get downstairs and into the passenger seat. I don't know how my mother gets into the back. I don't know anything at all.

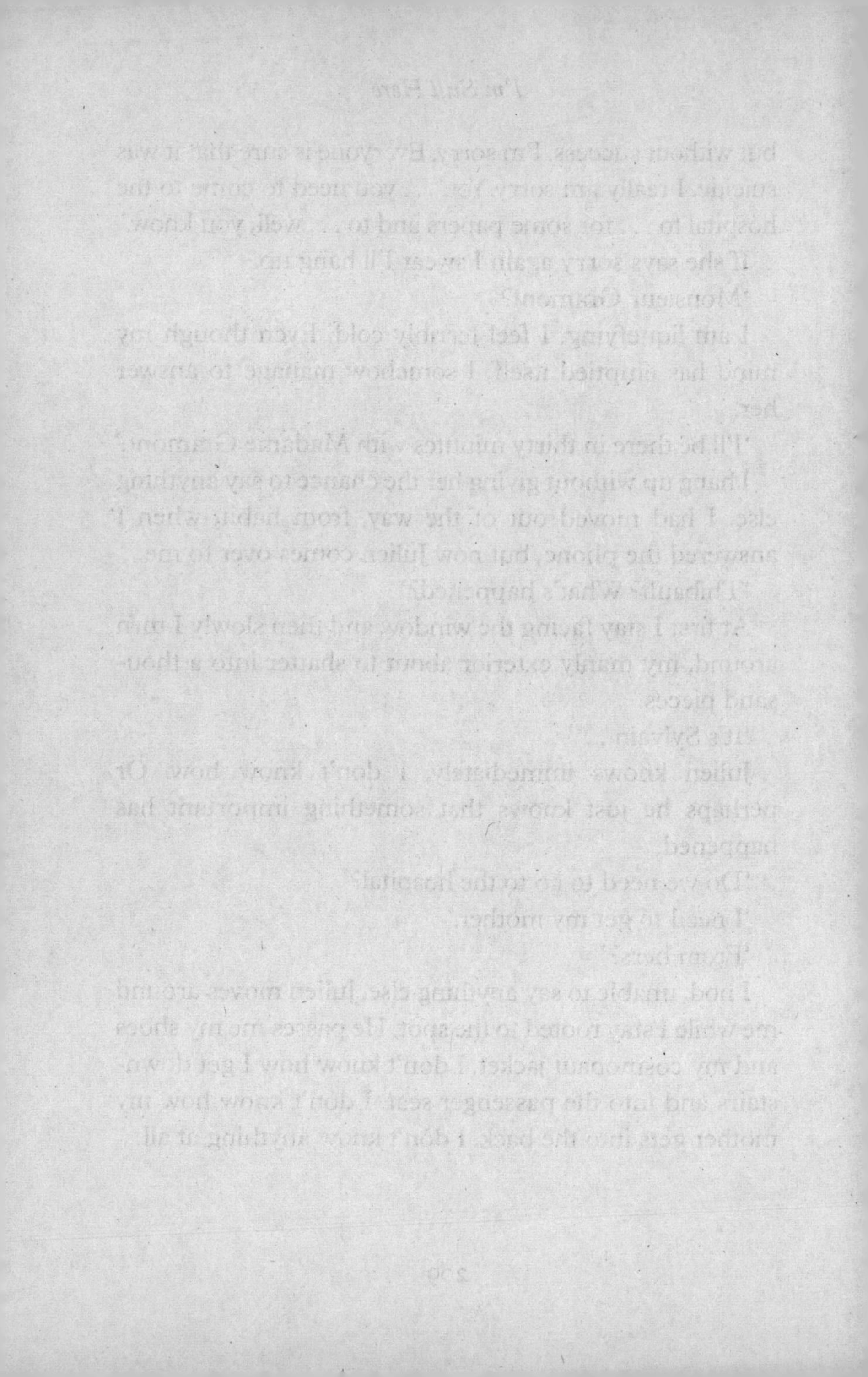

'Monsieur Grammont?'

'Your house?'

23

Elsa

He said, 'See you tomorrow.'

That was almost a week ago.

I've been through his last visit in my head a thousand times to see if I misunderstood something, but no. I'm certain he said tomorrow. At first I was quite calm. Perhaps he had something else to do. He *clearly* had something else to do. That didn't stop me feeling a little jealous. There was a glimmer of hope during the week, when I heard the door handle squeak, but it was only a doctor. I'm not quite sure which one, but I think it was my house officer. I think he looked through my notes and scribbled something. He also lingered beside all my screens, studying them apparently, and then he went out again without a word. But why should he speak?

So I've experienced some new emotions. Disappointment, fleeting bursts of anxiety. Fear.

That last one was bound to arrive at some stage. But I would have liked to have left it until the end. It wasn't the kind of fear that I wanted to feel.

On the glacier, when I had crampons on my feet and I saw a snow bank or a crevasse, I was always a little bit afraid. But it was a controlled, adrenaline-fuelled fear, as

I said to Steve. We knew that it all depended on us and on our handling of the situation; the way we crossed, our finesse as climbers, our efficiency, our agility and our intelligence. There was always an element of chance but really no one participates in that sort of climb without acknowledging the risk they're taking with every step.

What I feel today is a fear that devours me from the inside. I have absolutely no control over it, no way of smothering it beneath any other emotion. I'm under attack, and it is interminable.

First I was afraid that Thibault would never come back, so my mental exercises would be less effective, and I wouldn't wake up in time. Then, I was afraid that something had happened to him. Through all of this I had no doubt that my body would start working again. But now I'm not so sure.

Luckily that had the effect of stimulating things a little. My sense of touch comes back occasionally. I also think I may have perceived a vague scent of jasmine when the care assistant squirted it on my neck the other day, but I can't tell whether that information was real or just an effect of my imagination. Once again I decided to believe that it was real. If I'm going to die, I want to store away as many different types of information as possible, whether that means actually sensing the smell of jasmine, or just inventing it.

I feel like a bag filling itself with an assortment of things, some real, some artificial, some beautiful, some grotesque, all tangled up in each other. I can't distinguish or classify all the information that assails me any more.

There is more and more of it and it's as though my brain is arriving at saturation point. As though the active zones only cover a few nanometres squared, and these last three weeks have used all the space available. They stack themselves up and superimpose themselves onto each other and I am terrified that they'll all end up blending into one another. That's why I tell myself every day that I might be wrong, that it could be less than a week since Thibault said, 'See you tomorrow.' But the cleaning lady's radio confirms the date each night.

And it's strange, because my sister didn't come on Wednesday either. Maybe she had exams. Maybe that last visit shook her too much. I don't have much hope that anything will have happened with Steve. He definitely isn't a part of the swarm of boys that follows her around. I hope she gets there though. Steve deserves a proper love story, and she ought to be the one to share it with him.

I would have liked one for myself.

I think it is at once both absurd and essential to think like that. In my state, how can I possibly attribute such importance to my love life? I should just want to live, to be able to move, to get back onto a glacier, see my family, meet other people, discover the world, and to smile endlessly, and laugh at the sheer miracle of being here. I know that those are the important things. Enormously important. But being in love is what adds colour to all of that.

I smile in my head. I could teach my sister a thing or two about colours now. I could help her with her Fine Art. I wouldn't wish a coma on her to learn all that I have learned, but I'd like to share the insight with her. I don't know if she'd be able to adapt it to the real world with paint and brushes, but it would certainly be worth a try.

There I go – I'm starting to distract myself again. I need to stop thinking. Or at least to stop thinking about so many things at once. About so many people. It muddles me.

I found a solution yesterday – well, during the time span that I think was yesterday. I had already had it for a while, but I hadn't realised how much this little activity allowed me to forget everything else and eased my mind. So, I'll try it again now.

I want to turn my head and open my eyes.

I want to turn my head and open my eyes.

Occasionally a furtive thought tangles itself up in this. An 'I want to love', which I chase away immediately, before it develops into a much more harmful digression.

I want to turn my head and open my eyes.

Even if it doesn't happen until half a second before my mind switches itself off once and for all, I want to turn my head and open my eyes.

24

Thibault

The sound of a door banging on the landing makes me jump. With difficulty, I open my eyes and let them adjust to the darkness.

In a corner of the room, the digital clock display shows 02:44. I can hear the liquid murmur of the fridge in the kitchen, and the hum of one or two cars in the road below. Red lights from the room's electronic appliances glow here and there through the darkness, and the orange streetlights let some light in through the window.

If I didn't have this leaden feeling of pressure in my stomach, I might think it was an ordinary, calm night, and that I'd fallen asleep on my sofa reading something. Except that there's no book lying on the table, only the outline of a dead bottle of pineapple juice, and I think it must be two days since I last showered. Or maybe three . . .

I push away the old blanket with my foot and get up, circling my head to get rid of the crick in my neck. I think it's been at least twenty-four hours since I last ate. In fact I'm not even sure exactly how long it's been since I last moved from the sofa.

Better not to think about it. My stomach tightens. I can't work out whether I'm hungry or not. Either way, it would be sensible to eat something.

I get up and move towards the kitchen. My fridge is still relatively full, but the first things I take out of it are either out of date or unappetising. In the end I opt for steak haché with pasta. At almost three in the morning I don't have much imagination. I put some water on to boil and get the pasta ready on the side. The pan begins to heat up and I throw in the piece of meat. In a daze I get out the sieve, some cutlery and a plate and then I collapse into a chair.

I do all this in the dark, with only whatever weak illumination the streetlights offer to guide me around the landmarks of my kitchen. I don't know what it's like to eat in darkness, but I don't think I'll experiment with it now. I lean back in my chair to flick on the light over the hood of the cooker. My arms are just long enough to reach the little switch. The yellow light shines onto my back, but emits enough of a glow to be able to distinguish the features of my environment. That'll do.

Another little light, white and flashing, attracts my attention in the living room. It's my phone. I haven't been near a phone for several days. I even took the trouble of changing the landline answerphone message so that it says to leave a message if there's anything really important and that I'll listen to it later. Otherwise, people can just hang up. I can remember hearing my mother a couple of times, asking how I was. Julien and Gaëlle too. But, other than that, nothing since the first day.

I don't want to check my mobile phone yet. I'm not tempted to send one of those universal messages to all my contacts to explain the situation. There must be about thirty notifications on there. Between the text and answer-phone messages there'd probably be enough to keep me occupied for an entire morning. As well as the messages from my mother and Julien, I expect there are also some from other members of the family who, horrifyingly, probably want to talk about Christmas gatherings, which must be taking place in a few days' time. I think my cousin has been trying to get in touch since I saw him last Saturday.

Behind me the water boils. I get up to put the pasta on and turn the steak. The smell is already making my mouth water, and I reassure my stomach that it won't be long now. It's strange how our most primitive instincts can break through when we least expect them. I am consumed by the death of my brother yet my body still demands that I eat. It seems wrong to be able to feel hunger, but it's just the natural cycle of things. Life does go on.

That's also what the person who buried my brother last Saturday said. Everything is a cycle. We are born, we live, we die. It's cyclical, and it continues for us all until we are removed from the cycle in our turn. I'm not sure where I started, but I certainly feel caught in the middle of something with no way out.

But of course I know exactly where I started: last Thursday when I arrived at the hospital with my mother and Julien. It was obvious immediately that it had been no accident, that my brother had actually committed suicide. He had left various indicators in his room, one of which was addressed to me. When we were kids we had said that one day we would be airline pilots and that the two of us would fly together. There was a paper aeroplane left on his bed and on it he had written: 'We used the same runway but we both flew off on our own routes.' Underneath it he had drawn a smiley face and, even if there seemed to be an element of reproach in the way he summed up our lives, I knew that my brother was just speaking in a simple way about the different choices we had made for ourselves.

After that everything happened without me really noticing. The papers, the burial, my boss granting me two weeks of compassionate leave, Clara's christening where no one spoke to me, because Gaëlle and Julien had warned them in advance. I managed to crack a smile when I had Clara in my arms for the signing of the register, but I left straight after the ceremony. I changed my answerphone message when I got back that day. And since then I've had no contact with anyone.

The smell of the cooked meat brings me back to myself. I pile everything onto my plate and put it down on the table. I'm surprised at the voracity with which I devour my dinner, or whatever meal it is. I empty a half-bottle of water and fill it again before returning to the living room. I don't know whether it's having eaten something, or whether it's just waking up at this hour, but I'm terribly sleepy all of a sudden. I fall back onto the sofa with, for the first time in several days, the definite intention of going to sleep. I don't even have time to count to three before the darkness envelops me again.

The next time, it's the doorbell that wakes me. I glance at the clock. It's almost 11 in the morning. My living room is flooded with light; I must have been in a deep sleep. The persistent shrill sound of the doorbell makes me wince and I call out a vague 'I'm coming' as I disentangle myself from the blanket.

Making use of the little mirror behind my front door for the first time in a year, I quickly try to bring some order to my hair. Apart from that, I am dressed – I've been in the same clothes for what seems like an eternity, but they're better than nothing.

I open the door with the firm intention of sending whoever it is immediately on their way with a few strong words, but hold back when I see my elderly neighbour standing on the other side of the threshold.

'Ah! You *are* here!' she exclaims. 'I didn't know whether you were on holiday or not, because your letterbox is absolutely full! I have taken the liberty of collecting the overflow. Here. And . . . I recommend you have a shower.'

She throws me a glance and I just stand there, stunned, as she returns to her apartment. It must have been her door I heard slamming at three in the morning. She has a surprising amount of energy for someone her age. And she certainly doesn't beat around the bush.

First I glance at the post she has just handed me. Nothing very important, so I put it all down in the living room. I hesitate between coffee and a shower, and then I opt for coffee, followed by a shower. It is a renewed hunger that eventually coaxes me out of the bathroom, and I find myself going through the fridge again. While my breakfast is cooking, I pick up the pile of post and try to take an interest in it.

I was right, there's nothing urgent here. They're all completely pointless letters. The blinking light on my mobile crosses my field of vision again, when I carry the post back into the hall. I tell myself that while I'm on a roll with the letters, I might as well get stuck into the phone messages as well.

I look quickly at the texts and send very brief answers to Julien, my cousin and my mother. I don't feel like calling anyone. Then comes the long list of voice messages, so I leave the phone on loudspeaker to listen to them all, shouting 'delete' every once in a while from the kitchen, while I check on my breakfast. I must have reached about message number twelve when a new voice begins to speak.

'Hello, Thibault. It's Rebecca. Do you remember, we met twice at the hospital? It might seem strange that I have your number, but I managed to get it from the hospital staff. I wanted to warn you – and Alex and Steve agree that it's the right thing to do. Elsa is going to be disconnected. That's it. The family are planning for it to happen in four days' time. I wondered if you might want to come and say goodbye, or something like that. You've got my number now, so please do give me a call if you'd like.'

My body and my brain spring back into action in a flash. I leap onto my phone to listen to the message again, fighting with the keypad. After a minute I manage to find the date of the call. Rebecca contacted me on Monday the 16th. If I believe the display on my phone, today is the 20th. It doesn't take me long to realise that 'in four days' time' is today. Then whatever is happening outside slows, and everything starts whirring inside my head.

I turn off the gas and hurry to find my things. I don't stop to tie my shoelaces or to put on my jacket. By the time I reach the car, I'm not even sure if I locked the door. The only thing I know is that I have been the biggest fool of all the fools on this planet.

How did I forget her? How could I have forgotten Elsa?

As I drive I realise that I didn't forget her – I stopped believing in her. My brother's suicide made me rethink everything I had thought about the fact that Elsa could hear me. Elsa was my safe haven as long as my brother was there. From the moment he left us, I felt as though Elsa had left me as well. Except that, in reality, it's me who left her. What a fool . . .

I know that she can hear me. I'm certain of it.

The question I should be asking myself right now is not 'How could I have been stupid enough to leave her?' but 'Why would they want to unplug her?'

And with this question I rush into the fifth-floor corridor, preparing myself for the argument I will surely have to have any minute now.

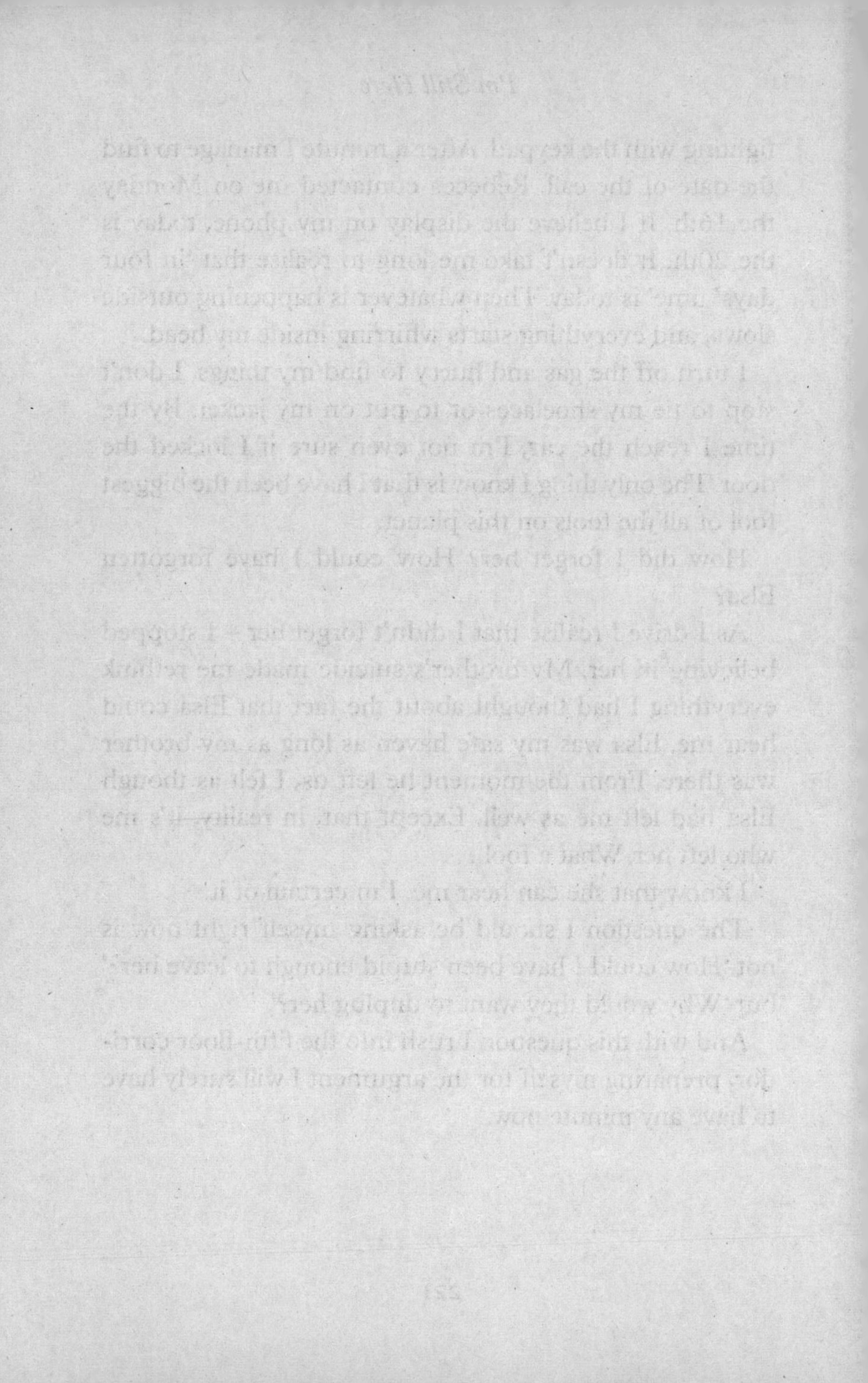

25

Elsa

I'm frightened.

That's obvious. In fact, I'm terrified.

By now I'm probably not the only one. It's been a long time since Loris and the consultant left. They only stayed for the beginning, the medical part. I feel like saying the electrical part, because, honestly, the switching off of all those machines could have been done by a six-year-old.

There are three people left in here with me now. There were nine of us at one point, me included, in this little room. It was quite crowded. Steve, Rebecca and Alex left a moment ago. I think I heard them say that they'd wait downstairs. It makes me sick just thinking about it. My friends waiting until I . . . the thought of it is horrifying. In their place I would run as far as possible; they've only been able to get five floors away.

My parents and my sister are here, and they are also waiting. I want to tell them to get out. I don't want their love, or their heartbreak. They've chosen not to believe in me and it makes me sick. But maybe they're right. What sort of life can it be, if you can only receive and never give anything? If I am destined to spend the rest of my days only listening and feeling, it might be better to—

The door opens. Sharp footsteps and deep, gulping breaths. My parents seem surprised, judging by the rhythm of their sighs, so it can't be the doctor come to announce that he's changed his mind.

'Hello,' says my mother in an infinitely sad voice. 'Have you come to see—?'

'Mum,' interrupts my sister, 'who do you think he's come to see? Come on, let's leave them alone for a couple of minutes. We've been standing here for an hour and a half already and there's been hardly any change, she's not going to go right this moment.'

The tone of her voice, firm but in immeasurable pain, overwhelms me.

'Why are you doing this?'

My heart leaps out of my chest, causing a slight alteration in my weakening pulse, but no one notices.

My rainbow.

I didn't recognise him from his footsteps or the way he was breathing, even though it's very quiet in my room now, with none of the racket from my respirator. Perhaps my brain really is starting to need oxygen; I've been breathing by myself for more than an hour, or at least trying to. My brain knows that it's getting more difficult, but I've been doing everything I can to keep going. Now that I can hear Thibault's voice, it's as though my body is really ready to hang on to a last hope.

My mother begins to stammer.

'What do you mean, why—?'

'Mum, you're unbelievable! Why are we disconnecting her? That's what he wants to know! Isn't it? Isn't that what you want to know?'

My sister's bitterness resounds through the entire room. She must never have agreed with my parents about unplugging me.

'Yes, that's exactly what I would like to know,' replies Thibault finally.

'Ask *them*!' my sister spits, before leaving the room.

'Pauline, come back!' calls my mother, weakly. 'I'll go and get her.'

'Leave her alone,' says my father.

'No, I'm going after her.'

The door closes. I imagine my father and Thibault standing together in the room. If the circumstances had been different, this would have been a very interesting meeting. But as things are, I sense that these are just two souls, each one as lost as the other. Thibault comes over and kisses my cheek. I imagine my father stiffening. He has no idea who Thibault is – neither do I, of course – and seeing a stranger kiss your daughter must provoke some sort of reaction.

'You're still breathing . . .' Thibault murmurs in my ear with relief, before straightening up. 'So?' he asks my father, without moving his hand from my shoulder.

'There is no hope,' says my father, sounding defeated.

'Because you have decided there isn't.'

'Do you think this decision has been easy?'

My father is beginning to get angry. I wish I could warn Thibault, but there's nothing I can do. So I listen. After all, I do it so well.

'It's easier than believing in her,' Thibault retorts. 'She can hear us! She knows that we're here! How can you sentence her to death?'

'Yes, I know all about people in comas supposedly being able to hear us. But eventually you have to face facts: Elsa has chosen to leave us.'

'She hasn't chosen anything at all! What choices can she make in this state?'

At this point, I actually want to tell Thibault he is wrong. I have chosen to try. The only trouble is that it hasn't worked in time.

'Who are you?' asks my father, suddenly.

'A friend of Elsa's.'

I know this answer by heart. I don't know why, but today I'm a little disappointed by it.

'I've never seen you before,' continues my father. 'Are you one of the ones who goes out to the . . . on those glaciers?'

That last word is spoken with such disgust that he must have grimaced while he said it.

'No. But we're wasting time. You cannot disconnect her. Not until she wakes up!'

'Elsa won't wake up ever again.'

'What do you know about it? I'm telling you that she can hear us!'

'It's just the way it is. And I don't have to listen to you, some so-called friend who I've never heard about, and who has no idea what my wife and I have been through to make this decision. I love my daughter. My wife and I love our daughter! How dare you come in here with your own ideas?'

By the time he finishes, my father is shouting. The volume of Thibault's voice contrasts with his. His response is almost a whisper.

'Because I am in love with your daughter.'

Feelings of hot and cold mixed together. Tingling in my fingers. The pulse monitor, the only one I am still attached to, reflects the accelerated beating of my heart. I hear Thibault turn towards me.

'Elsa? Elsa, I know you can hear me! Did you see that?' he calls to my father. 'She reacted.'

'Stop it. It's just a random discrepancy. Her doctors have explained all that to us. Please leave her now.'

My father's anger has turned to resignation.

'No chance,' says Thibault. 'I'm not moving from here.'

'Well . . . Do what you like. But . . . What are you doing?'

This time, I can hear the concern clearly in my father's voice. I also hear a noise in the background, the noise of my machines being moved around. I realise that Thibault intends to attach me to them again. But he doesn't know how to attach a drip, or where to put the nasal tubes.

'I'm doing what you should have done yourself,' says Thibault, concentrating on me.

'You're crazy . . . Stop it! Stop it right now!'

'Make me.'

Thibault's tone would have stopped anyone in their tracks. The rainbow has frozen into the haughtiest, most detached white-blue of any solid glacier I've ever seen.

'I'm going to get the doctors.'

My father moves away; the door closes. I am alone with Thibault.

He pushes around the machines, looking for the tubes. But the nurses have done their work too well. There doesn't seem to be anything much left in the room, except my respirator which is too heavy to move, and the pulse monitor, left here to pronounce the final outcome. I feel a trembling hand on my shoulder.

'Elsa, please. I know you can hear me. I don't know anything about what it's like to be in a coma, but I know you're here. Please . . .'

The door to my room opens with a lot of noise, but the sound reaches me muffled. I hear my father. I hear footsteps moving towards me. Or actually towards Thibault, because next they are pulling him off me. The sounds are growing more and more colourless. I can just make out the voices in the midst of this noisy, but also curiously silent throng. The consultant, the junior doctor, my father. My mother and my sister are hysterical. Steve is here too. He's talking to someone, screaming over them, even.

I feel light and heavy at the same time. I don't know where I am any more. Everything blends into everything else. So I go back to my exercises. Only once, though. Only once before everything fades away.

26

I ignored everything going on around me and just concentrated on her. My movements were automatic, my mind was focused exclusively on two things: getting myself free from Steve's iron grip, and watching her, watching Elsa.

If she stops breathing, I think I'll stop with her.

Now that I've stopped reasoning with them, all you can hear are grunts, breathing, murmurs. Some tears as well. Several of these may be coming from me. Who cares. But all of these sounds are regulated by the slow, terribly slow, beeping of the monitor.

The luminous curve hypnotises me. My eyes move from it to Elsa, conscious that, for the first time I am hearing her breathe naturally. She seems slowed down, fragile. With all the people surrounding me, watching me, I don't dare say a word. There are so many things I want to say to her. And at the same time, they could all be reduced down into a few words. I relax my shoulders; Steve's grip gradually loosens.

'You've got to let her go, mate.'

My head drops forward and my eyes fill with tears. My mouth endlessly repeats Elsa's name, so quietly you can hardly hear it, then I find my voice again with a last hope.

'Elsa, show them!'

I feel everyone's gaze turn to me.

The beep continues in time with her slowing pulse. My fists are so firmly clenched that my hands are completely white, and I begin a silent countdown. Ten . . . Nine . . . Elsa, wake up . . . Eight . . . Seven . . . Come on, I know you can hear me . . . Six . . . You reacted when I . . . Five . . . Four . . .

'What the . . .?'

The young woman's voice wakes me from my reverie. She must be Elsa's sister. Even though they look hardly anything like each other, there is something similar about them.

'It looks as though her heartbeat is picking up . . .'

I raise my head. She's right: the numbers on the screen are higher than they were the last time I looked. I turn my head to the doctors on my left. There's one who I recognise, the one who explained about all of Elsa's gadgets. They both look puzzled, but I think I can see a glimmer of hope in the eyes of the younger one. His superior shakes his head and whispers something in his ear. Then the junior doctor turns to the family.

'Random.'

That's all he says. I never want to hear that word again for the rest of my life.

Once. Just once.

It takes all the strength I have left in the active part of my brain.

I don't hear anything else. There's only one thing I want. Just once.

I want to turn my head and open my eyes.

My heart stops beating precisely as hers accelerates. I plunge into that stare, into the eyes I've only seen once. My lips find themselves engaged in a communal intake of breath with everyone else in the room. Everything is suspended.

I know that the hands on my watch continue to move, but the total motionlessness of everyone around me, including Steve, seems to stop time. I feel privileged; I am the only one who moves towards her.

I close my eyes. There was too much light. I open them again slowly and, at that moment, he is in front of me. I can't tell whether I preferred him as a rainbow or not, because my brain hasn't managed to distinguish all the visible colours yet. I just know that I've managed it, and his words echo my thoughts.

'You're here.'

I'm here.

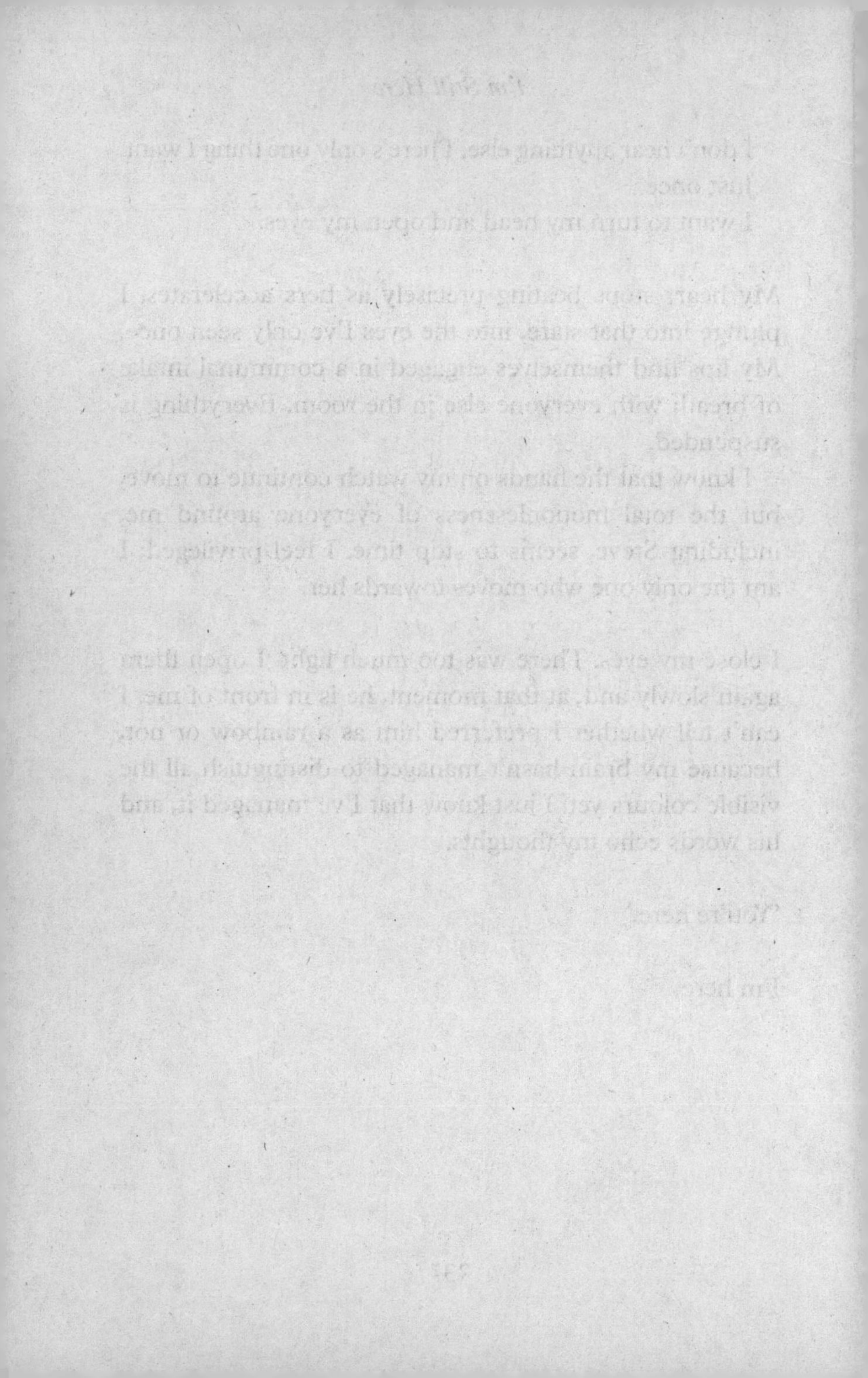

Acknowledgements

Writing my English acknowledgements was a dream . . . and now it's happening! Thanks to all the people who were here for me and for my book:

To my mum Annie and my best friend Hélène, who believed in me since the beginning.

To the wonderful teams at Hodder and Grand Central, who successfully took care of this story.

To a certain wizard at Hogwarts and his creator in the UK, who taught me English because of the dreadful six-month delay for the French translations. Without them, I would never have been able to write these words without the use of a dictionary!

And curiously enough, to a platform C at some train station near the sea . . .